Myths, Mothers, and Mystics

A SHORT STORY COLLECTION
SECOND EDITION

RUMER HAVEN

fallen·monkey

Also by Rumer Haven

Fallen Monkey Press

"She Who is Milk White" first published in *Beyond the Pillars:
An Anthology of Pagan Fantasy* by Bibliotheca Alexandrina, 2013
"Four Somethings & a Sixpence" first published by
Vagabondage Romance, an imprint of Vagabondage Press LLC, 2015
"The Glass Floor" used with permission of Brick Moon Fiction, 2017
"Revolve Her" first published in *Paperback Writers* by Locklear Books, 2019

First edition published by Fallen Monkey Press, October 2020
Second edition published by Fallen Monkey Press, July 2025

The characters and events in this book are fictitious.
Any similarity to real persons, living or dead,
is coincidental and not intended by the author.

ISBN: 978-1-0682293-0-5

10 9 8 7 6 5 4 3 2

Cover Design by RoseWolf Design
Interior Book Design by Coreen Montagna

Printed in the United States of America

To the Journey

Contents

Preface

Well. What to say about this little short story collection of mine…

For starters, I didn't set out to write it. Pretty much every piece in here wasn't a story burning inside me, demanding to be written. With the exception of "Reality TV," all of these stories were in response to external prompts: a creative writing exercise, themed calls for submission, a story contest, and a collaboration for charity.

Over the course of ten years, I wrote these stories at one point or another, for one reason or another. They were never meant to comprise a cohesive collection, so while there's technically a little rhyme ("Four Somethings & a Sixpence"), don't expect much reason. My standard tagline is "Fiction with a penchant for the past and paranormal," yet other than "She Who is Milk White," none of these tales are set in the past. "The Glass Floor" actually leaps into the future as my sole attempt at science fiction, and it's also the only one without supernatural elements (unless you count some highly questionable "science"). So, this isn't straight-up paranormal either.

It *is* all speculative fiction, though, and I should also take this opportunity to caution you: any otherworldly horrors aside, it's people who tend to be scariest, and, on that note, there's brief violence against women in "Bloody Hell, Mary!" and "Revolve Her." But I hope your main takeaway from those will be women coming into their own power.

However you want to look at the elements and themes of these stories, one guaranteed common denominator across this collection is, well…me. In a way, these stories reflect the journey I've taken as an author so far — from when I was cutting my teeth on a truly awful first novel attempt and had to blog my way out of writer's block, to when, three published novels later, I found myself right back in another writer's block with a book I'm still struggling to finish. I love writing long-form fiction, but I'm the first to admit I truly take ages to traverse that great distance from Chapter One to The End. So, it's short stories that lay the stepping-stones along that path, keeping me creative and curious and connected to my own writing whenever I'm stuck, uninspired, or editing others' stories instead.

A prolific writer I am not, but here's a sample of my random romps so far — with a living statue and a goddess, a woman and her mysterious mirror, a bride and her secret, a fertility executive and a lab scientist, ghost hunters and an innkeeper, and a tattoo artist and a tarot reader. Oh, and if you're still with me by the end, you'll see how I once got to corrupt young minds as keynote speaker at a high school literary festival.

At any rate, some of these stories you might've seen already, some you haven't. For better or worse, dear reader, you're seeing them now.

Rumer Haven

July 2025

Part I

Myth

She Who Is Milk White

A retelling of the "Pygmalion" myth.

I was already dwelling inside the stone when he "created" me. My outward form was different then, to be sure—rough, chipped, stained, weather-worn—but it was me. All along.

When I came into his possession, I enjoyed the way he would look at me, his eyes alight with the potential he saw, yet shaded in humility over what he'd actually achieve. He never doubted me, only his own ability.

From the beginning it was a labor of true love, the sculptor and I, he placing his hands upon me, circling me to summon what could come out, and I standing patiently, quietly, liking the way his hands felt. I might have felt cold to the touch, but he warmed me, his oils seeping into my pores to give me a luster I'd never outwardly known. He gazed at me so intently, caressed me so fondly.

And then he began chipping away.

In place of the soft beds of his fingertips and palms, I felt the rigid steel of his instrument, the chisel wearing me down from the outside in. I stood in mute terror as I watched my outer fortification crumble, pieces of me clattering to the ground like so much rubble. At the end of each day, he would clear the debris and thereby banish bits of what made me *me*. I had lost my natural coloring along with the scars of my environment and experience, and the ridges and dips that used to catch the warm rainfall were now smoothed and buffed into curves and mounds untrue to me. I would peer from my pedestal, beseeching him to look at and touch me the way he once had when he'd glorified me for what I was and could become, believing what we saw was the same. And still he would chip and hammer and chisel away.

Yes, I *had* loved him, and he'd loved me, but his spiraling admiration evolved into something foreign. As my figure slimmed and limbs emerged, I saw marble tendrils tumbling down my backside, coiling from what I supposed had become my "head," and what had been so raw and pure of my surface was sculpted into an imitation of silk that puddled at my "feet." The dust of my own decay choking my once porous flesh, I was stifled, and the more imprisoned I came to feel, the more he appeared to delight in the look of me.

In my state of paralysis, I looked on with no choice, in disgust of the way his ravenous eyes now consumed me, no longer meeting my gaze but gawking at the swells above my midsection and seeming to imagine what was concealed beneath the draping folds of my "gown." He would stare at me hungrily, fingering his tools as though contemplating whether he ought to just refine my stone away further and see what he really wanted to. At times, I felt he would. And it was at such times he would throw his implements down into my dust and approach me with his hands, in the way I had so long hoped he would again.

Yet his touch was not one of affection as he groped my swells, ran a finger down my curves, and forced his tongue onto what he'd sculpted to look like lips on me. Unsatisfied, he would fall away and moan and pull at his hair and raise a hand as if to strike me, only to sink to the earth among the gravel of my former self and weep over his unrequited physical love. I would not see him for days after spells like these, but he always did return, gawking anew and repeating the futile cycle.

When he'd determined he had "completed" me, he tested another means of seduction. He brought me gifts, laying them one by one at my feet in expectation that I'd yield to him, disregarding wholly that all I would ever accept from him was not what would die and disintegrate along with this mortal world, but that which would transcend the heavens into the infinite.

By this time, I had hardened to him. I was aloof, detached, even colder to his touch. I almost came to delight now in the way my new exterior would allure him, tease him, send him right back into pitiful despair. Once, in his most desperate of moments, I'd hoped he would affix his chisel to the heart that refused to offer me real love and drive it in to take his life as he had taken mine. Yes, this had become something I'd wanted badly, and I prayed to the gods that one of them would come to my aid.

And She did.

As the sculptor slept, snoring away in his miserable stupor, Aphrodite descended unto me, asking, "My dear Galatea, what is it you request of me?"

"I desire that you please take pity on poor Pygmalion lying there. Go to him, and bid him what it is *he* requests. He has endeavored so much to deserve what should come to him."

Aphrodite smugly responded, "I shall go to him, but I alone will determine the merits of his request."

"Fair enough," I conceded and left the goddess to take matters into Her own divine hands.

By sunset of the following day, as the sun bled red into the purity of a periwinkle sky, Aphrodite had given Pygmalion exactly what he deserved. I stepped off my pedestal, feeling the residue of my identity poking and scratching underfoot, and I allowed Pygmalion to hold me. I allowed him to marry me. And I allowed him to make love to me.

At first.

Coursing with the blood through my human veins was my human temperament, and I berated him for any way I deemed him lax in his vows. Intercourse led to weight gain when I conceived and bore our child, and I lifted not a finger to regain the figure he'd once bound me within. My aging skin became dry, calloused, and I turned an icy shoulder to him in the marital bed. The next strike of my hammer was to jealously forbid him from sculpting any more females. His livelihood impacted for the worse, he then resorted to whatever odd employment could provide for us, skipping his own meager meals such that his wife and son could have the more. It was still never enough, and you can be sure I informed him of as much at every opportunity.

Dejected and malnourished, he drank himself to near ruin and began to rot from within. The first organs to fail were his eyes, and I was lost to his sight forever.

That is when I felt the fissure, almost *heard* its sizzling crack.

Coursing with the blood through my human veins was now my human compassion, and I berated *myself*. The streaming corpuscles surged with strengthened force, eroding the rock that had calcified inside my chest until the fracture widened, deepened... and broke my heart.

I moved to sit beside him, to clasp my warm palm against his and press my fingertips into his sun-leathered skin, feeling the fine, frail bones of his hand. After a time, I lifted it to my breast so he could feel the gentle pulse that did beat there. I watched the subtle shifts and twitchings of muscle underlying his face, waiting for them to betray the pleasure he once took in laying his hands upon my curvature in this way. Watching, I waited.

All I detected was a slight furrow of the brow before Pygmalion released his hand from mine and raised it with his other to my forehead, to my temples, my cheeks, my jaw, my lips. From then on he would only touch my face to know my expressions, to pinch my chin with affection or to dry away my tears.

I liked the way his hands felt, and I emerged from the stone I had been dwelling inside when he loved me.

"She Who is Milk White" (the meaning of the name Galatea) was first written in 2010 as a creative writing exercise, taken from a book of prompts and posted on my blog. The aim was to tell a well-known fable, folk or fairy tale from an alternative point of view. In 2013, Bibliotheca Alexandrina published it in their Beyond the Pillars *pagan anthology, under the pen name CK Wagner. This was my first published story.*

Bloody Hell, Mary!

A retelling of the "Bloody Mary" legend.

Reflect

Mouth gaping as she stares into the mirror, Mary applies her mascara. Daytime makeup, so only one coat is necessary. Easy-breezy, just like the soft heather-grey tee slouching above her distressed jeans. She's only meeting him for coffee, after all. She can't let it look like any more than it is. She won't.

Butterflies betray her conviction from the inside. Their flittering wings scrape at her gut until memory coats them in bile, and they are subdued again.

It's only coffee, she reaffirms. *Nothing more.*

Mary plonks her mascara back into her makeup case and fingers out a tube of concealer. Passing on a second glass of wine last night was one of her better decisions — for so many reasons, but among them that she feels rested and hydrated today. So why the dark circles beneath the brown eyes staring back at her?

Grudgingly, she smears the concealer stick in half-moons and blends it with the pads of her ring fingers. She can do that much for Jack, she figures, knowing well enough it's foolish vanity she's appeasing in the end. Wouldn't be the first time. So maybe she should go with the lip gloss, too.

Dabbing some sticky shimmer to her lower lip, Mary blots it on a tissue and runs her other hand through her hair, mussing it a little, just enough to look effortless. She's pleased in spite of herself.

Clicking off the light, she leaves the bathroom and ultimately her apartment.

Clicking on the bathroom light, Mary is pissed. She glares at her reflection as she scrubs her palms vigorously under the faucet.

I dare you to smile, Mary, she says to herself. And the eyes that blink back at her seem to, even if the mouth doesn't. There's a glimmer to her irises and a fresh flush to her skin, so her frown looks out of place. She shakes it off, takes a deep breath, and pulls her shoulders back.

With a half-smile, she snorts. *Okay, getting stood up isn't the worst thing that could have happened. It was only coffee anyway.*

Three hours after she'd first left for the day, she's back home from her solo afternoon. She's sure the baristas were taking pity on her when they sliced up those free samples of fudge-nut brownies while she sat there by herself. Not that she'd never hung out alone at a café before, but this was probably the first time she'd arrived somewhere so sweaty and out of breath, twenty minutes late despite running from the bus stop. She paused two steps inside the door to scan all the tables before walking a lap and sitting at an available one, her knee bobbing up and down as her fingers tapped the table surface.

A tall, skinny guy walked out of the single-seater restroom. Too tall, too skinny, though—not Jack. So he really wasn't there. He must have been running late, too.

After ten minutes, she got up to order a bottle of water and an espresso so she didn't look like she was loitering. Not that she cared what people thought of her. Really, she was thirsty more than anything and needed her caffeine fix. Plus, when Jack finally did show up, it'd be clear she didn't wait for anyone. And from the diminutive size of her cup, she didn't intend to stay long.

If he showed up. As it was, he didn't.

She'd gotten the picture well before the second hour had passed, yet lingered for another coffee—large, filter, black—with an egg-salad sandwich and magazine.

Rinsing the soap off her hands now at her bathroom sink, Mary questions if Jack's pissed, too. Maybe he *had* been there but left when she was late. She should have stayed her course and taken the subway to meet him. Street traffic was already clogged by late afternoon, so she should've known not to veer off to the bus stop instead. But she did, and she can't change her mind now.

And maybe, just maybe, her subconscious had wanted to run late on purpose, hoping she wouldn't have to see him. Regardless, she'd given him two hours, but he couldn't give her twenty minutes.

Asshole. If she still had his phone number—thank God she'd never committed it to memory—she would text him as much. But she gave that the kiss-off long ago, along with her own digits. New life, new cell phone and provider. With an unlisted number. She needed a new phone anyway after the old one had smashed on Jack's windshield.

She supposes that giving him her new number when they'd first made the date—no, not a date, only coffee—could've helped avoid this mix-up, if that's what it was. But what if it wasn't? What if he really did just blow her off for the umpteenth time? And is she insane? Giving him that number would have entirely defeated the purpose. It would have defeated *her*.

So, everything has probably worked out for the best. Still, she looks back at the mirror and wishes she could wipe that smile off her eyes.

A week passes, and out of sight has proven out of mind as Mary applies her second coat of mascara with hardly any thought of Jack.

She knows by now that the effort he isn't worth is better directed at herself. The yoga class she started as distraction from her own thoughts has actually made her more in tune with them, surprising her to find that confronting her demons was the best way to exorcise them.

She's starting to feel relaxed and good in mind and body, inspiring her to try out a tight little black dress tonight. This girls' night has been on the calendar for ages, and it's worth a sparkle or two in her eye.

Yet when she assesses her reflection after that last sweep of her lashes, Mary steps back and pinches her brow. Her eyes look glassy, not glimmering, their whites a little grey and matted with red veins. And she used only a hint of liner and no mascara on her lower lids, yet inky black is smudged beneath them, as if she cried or sneezed while her upper lashes were still wet. She hates when that happens, not keen to spend any more time on primping and priming than she has to, but she knows this time she'd hardly blinked.

Mary reaches for a tissue and wipes the black from under her eyes, but it doesn't go away. Muttering curses under her breath as she glances at her wristwatch, she reluctantly pulls lotion and cotton pads from the cabinet and tries to remove the smudges that remain thoroughly stained in her skin. Her eyes look watery, probably irritated from the cream, so her last resort is applying more makeup to pretend she was going for a smoky eye. After that, she goes straight for the concealer—she's been sleeping enough, but those circles ringing her eyes still look so dark these days.

Mary brushes some powder above her cheekbones, fluffs her curled and lightly sprayed hair as she presses her lips to even out their gloss, then shuts off the light behind her.

Treading down the dark hallway in her pajamas, Mary giggles. She's still buzzing from a few cocktails, and every memory of girls' night strikes her as hilarious at the moment.

She flicks on the bathroom light and scurries in to relieve her bursting bladder. Sitting there, she leans forward and plops her chin into her hands as her elbows rest on her knees. She thinks of how her friends had seen Jack's "much cuter" doppelgänger leave the restaurant right before she arrived, and she wonders if it was actually him. If so, Mary mentally high-fives Fate for not crossing their paths again.

Naturally, she told her friends about the bullet she'd dodged at the coffee shop, and their frozen silence eventually melted into thank-Gods and good-riddances.

"He's bad for you, Mary," one of them sternly warned.

"You shouldn't have agreed to meet him in the first place," said another.

"You're not yourself when you're with him," said a third. Then they oohed and aahed over her new smoky-eye look.

Stepping up to her bathroom sink, Mary chuckles and rubs a hand down her cocktail-numbed face, eager for bed. It was a fun night but a long one in the end. Thanks to having to fix her makeup earlier, she'd arrived at the restaurant late, so she stayed late to compensate. Then when her subway line shut down for the evening, she spent forever trying to hail a taxi and ended up taking the night bus home instead. She'd almost caught that last train, too — the cuff of her coat sleeve caught in the subway doors when she'd reached to keep them from closing. All she accomplished was a sooty sleeve and wounded pride as drunken passengers watched her with amusement or apathy from inside the train car.

Mary can laugh about it now, though, from the warm comforts of home, and she does as she washes her hands. She shakes them out before turning off the faucet, then looks up and—

Gasps.

Rubbing her face a minute ago really did a number on her makeup, because her eyes are blackened, and her crimson lipstick has smeared up to her nose.

Mary looks like a bloody mess, like an evil clown, and she giggles at the ridiculous sight while she fetches cotton and cleanser from the cabinet. Despite her efforts, though, she can't wipe off the color, so she eventually gives up and goes to bed, hoping her pillow will do the work in her sleep.

A month later, Mary returns home from the gym. It's the Friday afternoon of a three-day weekend, and she's making it one of indulgence.

Once she showers and dresses, she's off again for a facial appointment, and after that, she's consulting someone at the department store cosmetics counter to learn what foundation and powders are best for her skin tone and type. And on her way home from there, she thinks she'll pop into a nutrition store for some vitamins or herbal supplements that could improve her complexion from the inside out.

Because the fact is, Mary hasn't been looking so well lately. She's not normally this fixated on appearance, but she's been eating healthy and taken up running again, jogging to and from work at least three days a week and taking yoga class twice. She feels at the peak of her physical fitness, and it's helped her focus better at work and manage stress. The only times Jack ever enters her mind are with a subsequent sigh of relief that she's never run into him again. For the first time in four months, she believes she's fully and truly over the bad business of their year-long relationship.

So why her face in the mirror should appear ever sallower, sometimes sunken, sometimes puffy—almost bruised—simply escapes her. Whether capillaries are bursting or she suffers a deficiency, Mary has also made a doctor's appointment for first thing tomorrow morning. Hopefully that will shed some light or at least provide a dermatologist referral.

In the meantime, her friends shake their heads with bemused expressions whenever she complains, fervently praising her beauty and gushing that she looks the best she ever has, that she needs to have more self-confidence. Then they ask if this has anything to do with impressing Jack, if Mary's been seeing him secretly, which Mary denies over and over again. So, she's simply stopped talking about her superficial concerns to avoid interrogation and sounding insecure, as if she's fishing for compliments.

In keeping it to herself, she just hopes today's remedies will work.

The next day, Mary trudges into the bathroom without bothering to turn the light on. She fishes in her cabinet for eye drops to soothe the sting of her tears.

Today's doctor's appointment has turned up nothing. She's still waiting on blood test results, but her physician otherwise insisted during the examination that none of her alleged symptoms were visible. With a shrug, he did indulge her claims with some benign conjectures and recommendations, which gave some solace but not enough to quell Mary's paranoia. She thinks about seeking a second opinion.

Eyelids closed, she looks up, down, and side to side, rolling her eyes around in the saline solution and breathing deep, slow breaths as she prays she's only imagining things. That the doctor is right and she'll open her eyes to the healthy vision he saw. With hands splayed on the countertop on either side of the sink, she hangs her head for a while. Her nose itches, so she brings her face to her left arm and scratches it against her inner elbow. The Band-Aid there from her blood sample scrapes her cheeks.

Please, Mary. Please, Mary. Please, Mary…

She raises her face to look at the mirror in the dark. Her reflection stands hunched over the sink, too, in silhouette. There's enough light from the hallway, though, for Mary to see the ends of her hair look stringy, almost wet in the way the strands congeal together. She swears she even sees a couple of beads of inky liquid drip from them to the sink, so she looks down at her actual tendrils where they hang past her shoulders. Of course, it's difficult to discern in the dimness, but by touch her hair seems smooth and brushed, not like she got caught in the rain.

Mary looks back up at her face and jolts a bit at the weird tricks of light and shadow playing upon it. A protrusion appears on her forehead, right beneath where her hair parts at the scalp, but when she lifts a hand to her head, she doesn't feel a lump there, not so much as a zit.

The rest of her face, though, is dark, so dark. She can't make out her nose or mouth, and her eye cavities yawn open like bottomless hollows.

A chill tickles down Mary's spine for just a moment before she decides to turn on the light and assess her features properly.

She reaches for the switch. But before Mary flicks it, she draws in a long breath and reminds herself that what the doctor said was *good* news, that she doesn't *want* something to be wrong.

She couldn't possibly feel more otherwise, after all, and she almost has her mystery malady to thank for it. She's made the lifestyle changes she needed to since the breakup, and as long as she's improving on the inside — mentally, emotionally, and physically — she shouldn't care how she appears on the outside.

Life has been good, really good, and she's the only one around her who hasn't seemed to realize that. No one else has viewed her as a freak, only her — a souvenir from the Jack days, it seems, back when he looked at her like she was some portrait of Dorian Gray, seeing ugliness and weakness where she couldn't, and *hadn't*, but started to under the crushing power of his suggestion.

Her friends are right, of course. Jack was awful for her, awful *to* her, and these months without him have given her the pleasure of meeting herself again. And what she sees in herself is pretty great.

Spreading her lips into a broad grin, Mary exhales and flips on the light.

She turns her head to smile at her reflection — and freezes for a few sickly seconds before her rigor mortis thaws into what would be a blood-curdling scream if she could only find her voice.

Clutching at her face and chest, she falls to her knees and vomits.

Rewind

Mouth gaping as she stares into the mirror, Mary applies her mascara. Daytime makeup, so only one coat is necessary. Easy-breezy, just like the soft heather-grey tee slouching above her distressed jeans. She's only meeting him for coffee, after all. She can't let it look like any more than it is. She won't.

Mary plonks her mascara back into her makeup case and fingers out a tube of concealer. Accepting that second glass of wine last night was not one of her better decisions—for a couple of reasons, one being that two drinks led to more. She looks better than she feels, but over the course of the day, the hangover will darken the circles under her eyes. Grudgingly, she smears the concealer stick in half-moons and blends it with the pads of her ring fingers. She can do that much for Jack, she figures. When they ran into each other at the bar last night, he commented even then that she looked tired.

But she apparently looked good enough for him to buy her that drink. She'd only intended to have the one after-work glass of wine with colleagues before going home to catch up on reading and laundry. Otherwise, it's difficult for her to stop after two, and isn't it just like the old days with Jack when she doesn't…

But old habits die hard, and in a moment of weakness, she gave Jack benefit of the doubt. No, she won't call herself weak—caught off guard sounds much better. Stumbling into the person you've been avoiding will do that. It even took her a couple of seconds to recognize him; he looks better than when she moved out of his apartment three months ago. He's gotten some sun and appears to have lost the beer bloat.

More surprisingly, he greeted her so kindly—not what she'd expected after leaving him with that cracked windshield. As a couple, no doubt they brought out the worst in each other, but maybe as acquaintances, they could find the closure Mary has been seeking. There's no harm in them just talking…a little. But nothing more than that. She needs today to make that clear.

Because Mary worries she might've led him on last night. As she could have predicted, she over-imbibed, but she assumed it was just a one-off encounter and wanted to make it as comfortable and amicable as possible. And in enjoying what had once been so good about them—Jack really could be so funny—perhaps she even got a little flirty with him. Blame it on the wine.

What she didn't anticipate, though, was that he'd ask what she was doing the next day. Everything sounded like a great idea by their third round last night, so she agreed to coffee this afternoon near his office. And today she hopes the arm's-length sobriety of sunshine and caffeine will set Jack straight on where things are *not* going between them.

Dabbing some sticky shimmer to her lower lip, Mary blots it on a tissue and runs her other hand through her hair, mussing it a little, just enough to look effortless. She's pleased in spite of herself.

Clicking off the light, she leaves the bathroom and ultimately her apartment.

Clicking on the bathroom light, Mary is confused but almost unnervingly excited. She glances at her reflection as she scrubs her palms vigorously under the faucet.

I dare you to deny it, Mary, she says to herself. And the sharp eyes that blink back at her do seem to snub the idea that there was any connection with Jack at the coffee shop. She knows she should believe them, too.

If only Jack wasn't so punctual, so courteous, so clever all afternoon. She could have sat there for hours, genuinely enjoying his company and handsome golden looks made more rugged by a closely trimmed beard.

People don't change as easily on the inside, her reflection seems to warn her, its countenance looking angry more than anything, and Mary frowns, considering how funny body language can be sometimes, when doubt can tug desire into a twisted, almost spiteful submission. She shakes it off, takes a deep breath, and pulls her shoulders back.

With a half-smile, she snorts. *Okay, okay. I know. Tread lightly with this one. It was only coffee anyway.*

Three hours ago, she'd been debating whether to take the bus or subway when the bumper-to-bumper traffic finally swayed her toward the train. She arrived at the café ten minutes early, cool, collected, and placing bets with herself that Jack would be late, as usual.

But not two minutes afterward, there he was — he paused just two steps inside the door to scan all the tables before approaching the one where she sat. She hadn't ordered yet, so he went to the counter on both of their behalves, insisting on treating her. He remembered how she takes her coffee black, and even came back with a fudge-nut brownie for her — an impetuous gesture like during their first weeks dating, not the months to follow when he'd made her swap calories for self-control.

Rinsing the soap off her hands at her bathroom sink, Mary questions again if Jack enjoyed her company, too. She knows they didn't have much time — he was called back into his dental office for an emergency twenty minutes later. Had she been at all late, she might have missed him entirely.

But there was no sense in analyzing the what-ifs; it was enough to see that last night hadn't been a fluke. Today, they got on really well, and she knows it's ridiculous, but the abrupt end to their coffee date—no, not a date, only coffee—left her wanting more…

Asshole. Thanks to her less-than-best efforts, she's let him in again, even if only into her thoughts. That's the only kink her armor needs to undo three months of fortification. His sudden departure from the café had thrown her off, too—by just enough that she agreed to quickly exchange contact details. Now he had her new, unlisted phone number.

Time to disconnect another one… but maybe not. Not until she gives him a fair chance to call her. Just once. Just to see if he will at all.

So, everything has probably worked out for the best. Still, she looks back at the mirror and wishes she could see a smile in her eyes, not the distrust that dulls them.

A week passes, and out of sight has not proven out of mind as Mary can't even apply her second coat of mascara without thinking about Jack. Thank goodness it's girls' night tonight.

She feels bloated but looks surprisingly svelte in her little black dress, and she's bravely experimenting with a smoky eye. She hopes it will camouflage what her concealer probably doesn't. She doesn't look tired in her reflection, but she knows she is; she hasn't been sleeping enough—her dreams invaded by shit men who don't call when they promise to—so the lighting must be doing her skin justice. Jack always pointed out how dark her eye circles would get after too much wine or too little sleep, or a frequent combination of the two.

The heavy eye makeup is bolder than she's ever attempted, but it makes for a fun distraction. Besides, if she botches it up, she knows her gals won't judge. And if she does it just right, she wonders what Jack would think of the change…

There she goes again. She knows he isn't worth the mental energy and could kick herself for giving an ounce of it. Between her work, friends, and piles of books beckoning her from the shelves, life has managed to fill in the blanks he left behind, and the last thing she wants is for the other week's drinks and coffee to perforate it with spaces again. She knows from last time how Jack can overtake that space, filling and expanding beyond it to rip her life. And she knows it's in those spaces that the demons like to hide.

There's not room enough behind her eyes for those demons and her tears. One by one, the little fiends poke the teardrops with their pitchforks, bursting them so the water drains down Mary's face as she slumps toward the sink. Pressing both lips and lids together, she lets her face crumple, and her lungs hyperventilate for a few solid shakes.

Damn you, Mary. You're stronger than this. Pull it together.

She claws the countertop and deeply inhales, inflating her torso to stand up straight and assess the damage to her smoky eye. Opening her lids, she braces for the hideous black-widow-spider streaks. In fact, before she even looks, Mary reaches for a tissue and bottle of cleanser to wipe the black from underneath her eyes.

But when she faces the mirror again, what she sees instead is…striking, actually, if that's not too conceited for her to admit. Her eyes are glimmering, not glassy, their whites white and not matted with red veins. The inky black of her mascara and liner is almost perfectly intact; her upper lids are artfully shadowed, and what she applied to her lower ones is diminished but not smudged.

Glancing at her wristwatch, she heaves a sigh of relief that now she won't be late. As her finishing touches, Mary brushes some powder above her cheekbones, fluffs her curled and lightly sprayed hair as she presses her lips to even out their gloss, then shuts off the light behind her.

Treading down the dark hallway in her pajamas, Mary groans. She's wasted from too many cocktails, and all she wants to do is pull the trigger at the toilet so she can evacuate the devil liquid from her body and return to bed to pass out.

"Never could handle your liquor," Jack calls from the kitchen. Mary can hear her cabinets opening and slamming shut, glasses clinking, and she knows he'll be disappointed when he finds no snacks or alcohol in the apartment. "You've got beet juice but no beer? Senior citizen isn't sexy on you, Mary."

And there it is. But she can't bother with him now, not until the bathroom stops spinning and she can walk her way back down the hall. She's crumpled on the floor, in the dark, and as she spits the remaining moisture from her mouth, a shadow falls over the shaft of light beaming in from the hall.

"You all right?" Jack asks from the bathroom doorway. "C'mon. Let's go to bed." He reaches out to her, and she rises from the tile to take his hand and let him lead her to the bedroom.

Blinking through a cottony haze, Mary can't quite process her reality. What was supposed to be a carefree night out with the gals began with three of her closest friends making a beeline for her as soon as she'd walked in the restaurant door.

"We think Jack's here," one of them said, guiding Mary by the arm to the ladies' room. "Did you know this?"

"Do you want to leave? We can leave," said another.

Dumbstruck, Mary just shook her head to both questions and inwardly gave Fate the middle finger for crossing their paths like that again. Jack could be on a date for all she knew, and her friends looked ready to have at him.

"Probably stalking you," said the first, rolling her eyes before she narrowed them. "Are you okay? Have you been crying?"

"I'm fine." Mary must have been kidding herself earlier that her makeup looked okay, definitely a trick of her bathroom's bad lighting.

"But your mascara—"

"I'm *fine*," she snapped, but not sooner than one of the young women had already brought a wet paper towel to her face. Huffing, Mary said thanks and allowed her friends to play beauty parlor since she obviously didn't trust her own judgment anymore.

Eyes widened and rolled up to the ceiling as the coarse paper chaffed beneath her lower lashes, Mary reiterated to her friends that it was nothing and she didn't want to talk about it. Could they just have the fun they came for — no boys allowed. The rest of her face was touched up in silence. Once finished, they wasted no time relocating her to a bar around the corner.

A couple of drinks later, Mary's phone went off. The number looked familiar, but the caller was unknown.

"Hello?"

"Where are you? I thought I saw you before."

Him.

"Out with friends."

"Can I meet you somewhere later?"

He could. Mary had just firmed up the details and hung up when she heard, "He's bad for you, Mary."

"You shouldn't have agreed to meet him," said another friend.

"You're not yourself when you're with him," said a third.

She played dumb and lied that it was someone else, a cute co-worker who'd been flirting with her lately. They didn't seem to buy it but kept their peace for the remainder of their time together.

By ten, Mary made her excuses to leave. She met Jack at his favorite club, and a few stiff drinks and drunken PDAs on the dance floor later, here they are. At her apartment, an address Jack now knows. Hand in hand, heading to her bed. He practically took her in the cab already on their way home, right there on the backseat — until it came time to let her pay the fare.

Mary thinks she has to puke again. She pauses just inside her bedroom doorway, a hesitation she knows he won't honor, not this far into it, not in this state.

With slow steps, Jack rotates and backtracks toward her, backing her out of the doorway and against the hallway wall. Still holding her hand, he seizes her other one and brings both above her head, pinning them there as he presses his mouth against hers. He smears his lips all around Mary's and tries to penetrate them. But she can still taste bitter-sour stomach acid on her tongue, and when it reluctantly meets his, Jack snaps his head back.

He lets go of her to wipe his mouth. "Brush your teeth first." Licking at his lips, he looks down at his fingertips, pinches his brow, and then wipes off his mouth again before gliding his forearm under his nose as though for good measure. "Some things don't change, I see," he mutters under his breath as he pivots to disappear into the bedroom.

Hands back down at her sides, Mary clenches them into fists. She feels her nose running and wipes it with her knuckles. Then she returns to the bathroom to do as she was told — only because she knows if she waits long enough, Jack will be snoring once his head hits the pillow.

Biding her time, she stands at the sink and rigorously rubs her face, not caring if it smears her makeup all over. Dropping her hands, she jolts at the blood on her palms.

She's prone to nosebleeds, especially after drinking when she's dehydrated. Jack mashing his face against hers a moment ago couldn't have helped. He must've noticed that just now but didn't say anything. *Jerk.* Mary yanks off some toilet paper to plug the offending nostril.

With her head tipped back until the bleeding stops, she tries to brush her teeth. She feels around on the countertop for her toothbrush and toothpaste and then holds the two up together in the air so she can see what she's doing as she applies paste to the bristles. Setting the toothpaste down, she plucks the tissue out of her nose before lowering her face and —

She squints at the mirror. Rubbing her face earlier did hardly anything to her makeup, and there's not so much as a speck of red beneath her nose when she'd expected to look like a bloodied clown.

What she does see is a merry twinkle in her eyes, and Mary wonders if there's something inside her that hasn't given up yet. She'd almost laugh if she didn't want to cry, and she prays for peaceful sleep after she slips into bed beside a snoring Jack.

A month later, Mary returns home from Jack's. It's the Friday afternoon of a three-day weekend, and she wants a fresh change of clothes for tonight. Naturally, Jack's first nights crashing at her place were just a novelty, and, soon enough, he played the *but-my-place-is-closer-to-everywhere* card that got her walk-of-shaming all over again.

Once she showers and dresses, she's off again to his place, picking up fresh food and flowers along the way. A last-minute dental appointment summoned Jack into the office for a few hours, so while he's away, Mary has plans to tidy his apartment and prepare a healthy dinner for his return. She wants everything to be as nice and friendly as when they first reunited so she can let him down easy.

Because the fact is, Mary hasn't been doing so well lately. She's not normally this distracted at work or dishonest with friends, and she realizes she's slipped into the bad habits of her past.

Before Jack reentered her life, she'd gotten so close to feeling fully and truly over the bad business of their year-long relationship. The mood swings, the lies, the low self-esteem — none of that had plagued her anymore, and while she thought she'd realized it the first time around, now she sees the capital-T truth with undeniable, chastening clarity:

It's not her, it's him.

And, oh, it's been him, again and again and again. Keeping her holed up inside even on the most gorgeous of weekends, first to screw around in bed all day and now to watch TV and subsist on takeout. Talking her out of plans with her friends, first by giving her gifts and now guilt trips. Wearing her down with his sweetness and neediness and sexiness and explosiveness.

Because the explosions do happen, just as they did before. The silly fights he instigates in the heat of a drunken moment, the ones that escalate for no good reason and are instantly — supposedly — regretted in the morning. He'll grab at her wrists and shake her or seize her mouth to keep it shut when she tries to argue back. For the last week, her jaw has been clicking, and Mary swears it's from their last late-night bout.

That, or the make-up sex they had afterward. In the throes of possessive passion, Jack has taken to sucking and biting at her body to the point of pain, and her cheeks and mouth have been no exception. She knows where this will lead, because she's seen it all before.

So why her face in the mirror should appear ever clearer, always glowing — never bruised — simply escapes her. It seems to tell her that she should be happy, that she *is* happy…somewhere and at some time, but not here. Not now.

But she *could* be, couldn't she? The confident-looking, fresh-faced woman who looks back at her every day in the mirror is the person she wants to be on the inside, too. She thinks — she *knows* — she can be that Mary if she doesn't give up on her. If she hasn't given up already.

In the meantime, her friends — when they do see her — shake their heads with mystified expressions over what in the hell she got herself back into. They say they want to be there for her, but she makes it difficult when she's repeatedly a fool for this guy. So Mary has simply stopped talking about it to avoid interrogation and wait until she sorts it out on her own.

In keeping it to herself, she just hopes tonight's remedy will work.

The next day, Mary trudges into her bathroom without bothering to turn the light on. She wets a washcloth under cold water, then brings it to her face to soothe her stinging eye.

Last night's dinner didn't go quite as she'd hoped.

What *did* go to plan was a spotless apartment infused with the warmth and spice of a slow-cooked vegetable tagine on the stove.

A kitchen table topped with linen, a vase of lilies, and a chilled bottle of prosecco. Mary was very careful to buy just the one bottle, enough to fortify her nerves and relax Jack's. But nothing more.

Jack doesn't much care for sparkling wine anyway, so she'd anticipated that whatever he did drink would be choked down reluctantly. She had hoped it would encourage him to favor the water she'd also set out on the table, iced and enticing in a clear glass pitcher with lime slices floating on top. The rest of his liquor, she'd dumped down the drain.

Eyelids closed, Mary breathes deep, slow breaths as she prays she's only imagined what just happened. That what transpired last night is where it really ended, not this nightmarish carryover into today. With one hand splayed on the countertop while the other presses the cloth to her eye, she hangs her head over the sink for a while.

Last night when Jack returned home from work, he found Mary smiling if a little anxious. He inhaled and complimented the aroma in the air before saying it was about time she did some cooking. When he asked what was in the dish, he grimaced first at her answer and then at the prosecco on the table.

"No meat? What, are you vegan now? Is this more Goop shit to go with that yoga class you keep saying you're gonna take?" He'd said it jokingly yet injected the air with a familiar tang that bit at the back of Mary's tongue.

She held her smile. "It's good for us. Now just have a seat and unwind from your day."

It was all very Suzie Homemaker while she served up their food and sat to enjoy their meal. Until she didn't. Jack was a lot of things, but he wasn't stupid, and they'd barely moved on from their salads to the tagine when he asked her point-blank what all the fuss was for.

She didn't answer right away, not prepared for it to come up so soon and realizing that it wouldn't go down at all the way she'd rehearsed it.

Her stuttering, blushing hesitation was fertile ground for speculation to grow. Gripping his cutlery and pumping his fists around it like two raging, beating hearts, Jack launched his accusations.

She was pregnant, wasn't she. Bet she did it on purpose, too, poked holes in the condoms or something to force him into commitment. And of course at a time when his practice was doing so well. Eager to play the role of doctor's wife, was she?

No?

Well, it figured. He wouldn't give her credit for being that manipulative anyway, let alone actually managing to pull it off.

So then, if it wasn't that, she must be cheating. Trying to ease her conscience and deflect suspicion by pampering him so much. But, again, she wasn't that clever. He could see right through her. And when he found that asshole loser, he'd cut his dick off and stuff it in a jar. Who was the guy?

"No one."

"Mary, who is he?"

"Someone who doesn't exist, because I'm not cheating on you! I wouldn't do that! You know I wouldn't."

Running his thumbs along the slim edges of his knife and fork, Jack said nothing for a few beats, just hissed air out of his nose until the corner of his mouth quirked up in a smirk.

"Couldn't, more like," he said.

"Wouldn't."

He snorted. "If you could score anyone else, then why were you still single after we broke up?"

"Why were you?"

His sneer tightened into a frown, and, slowly, he placed his utensils back down. Reaching for the prosecco, he poured more into his as-yet-untouched flute, topping it off to the brim, and then he downed the entire glassful. He repeated the action once more before discarding the flute altogether and just clutching the bottle.

"What's going on?" he asked quietly after a while. "Mary, what is it really?"

Sitting slumped in his chair, his fingertips nervously twitching against the bottleneck and picking at its foil, he at last looked defeated, almost boyish and scared. Almost sincere and vulnerable enough for Mary to feel a pang of endearment, guilt. Regret, maybe.

Almost.

She closed her eyes and envisioned herself as the woman she saw in the mirror. Drawing a fortifying breath, Mary opened her eyes, looked at Jack directly, and answered him honestly.

He just sat back in his chair and wiped his mouth with a napkin.

Then, with a solemn expression and his watery eyes trained on the table, he said in a low voice, "Please leave." Mary spoke up to offer an apology and more explanation, but he cut her off with "It's done. Just go."

And so she did.

Mary now raises her face to look at her bathroom mirror in the dark. Her reflection stands hunched over the sink, too, in silhouette. There's enough light from the hallway, though, for her to see her hair looks unfathomably dry, smooth and brushed, not wet and stringy, which she *knows* it is from what just happened. She can feel it, right now, with her fingers.

Please, Mary. Please, Mary. Please, Mary…pull yourself together.

She looks back up at her face and inspects the way light and shadow play upon it. She sets the washcloth down and brings her hand back up to gently rub the lump on her forehead that she feels is there even if she can't see it.

The only time Jack had hit her before was over four months ago, right before she'd stormed out of his apartment with a suitcase and flung her cell phone at his car parked out on the street. He'd delivered a slap that felt like a hot frying pan, but this time… this time, she understood that expression about seeing stars.

When she left his place for the final time last night, she expected a delayed reaction would eventually bring him back with all guns blazing; he was never one to go down without a good verbal sparring. And when he buzzed up to her apartment late this morning, the tightness in his voice over the intercom confirmed that.

What she couldn't sense until she'd let him into her home, though, were the fumes of stale liquor rising off his breath with every word he could muster. An all-night bender to follow that prosecco, Mary assumed, judging by the same clothes he'd worn at dinner.

His speech was slurred but started out sedate. He'd been lost without her before, and he couldn't lose her again. He refused to.

Talking became pleading, then pleading became crying, and crying became yelling, and when yelling turned into screaming, Mary's cries rang out against the beat of a neighbor pounding against her door.

Whoever had run to her rescue, however, wasn't in time before she'd already taken a couple of solid blows.

But she didn't beg for mercy. Mary was too weak to fight Jack back in body, but she found strength in mind, and she let him back her into a corner in the kitchen — right into the nook of her L-shaped countertop, where her coffee had finished brewing.

With one arm protecting her battered face, Mary reached back with the other. She seized the handle of her coffee pot and splashed the hot black liquid in his face. On her next swing, she crashed the pot down on his skull.

Coffee and glass rained on her, too, but, numb to it, she just watched as Jack groaned and backed off, right into the aim of her neighbor, who'd finally let herself in through the unlocked door, pepper spray in hand.

That woman is still sitting on Jack now, right where she pinned his semiconscious self to the coffee-stained carpet — finishing the job Mary had started. They're all waiting in silence for the police to arrive while Mary cleans herself up in the bathroom.

Stepping away from the sink, she reaches for the bathroom switch to finally turn on the light. Before she flicks it, though, she draws a long breath and reminds herself that what just happened was a *good* result compared to what could have gone even more horribly wrong.

But it didn't, and she has her mystery mirror to thank for it.

She's made the change she needed to, if a little late, and life still has a chance to be good, really good. It took her own reflection to help her realize that. All those warning gazes and glimpses at what life could look like have reminded her that she knows better, she *is* better, and she feels like she's meeting herself again. And what she sees in her potential is pretty great.

Spreading her lips into an unexpected grin, Mary exhales and flips on the light.

She turns her head to smile at her reflection — which stares back at her with two wide-open eyes even though she knows one of her eyelids is now swollen shut. She watches her reflected self clutch at her face and chest, then fall to the floor.

But Mary on this side of the glass feels fine. Stands tall. Closing the bathroom door for privacy, she steps closer to the mirror and waits patiently.

Reset

Having emptied her stomach down to the bile, Mary gives one last good spit before breathing deeply and bracing to look back at the mirror.

Willing her knees to support her legs again, she scrapes her feet against the tile to curl into a squat and then rises to standing. She wipes saliva from the corner of her mouth and stares her reflection down once again.

Maybe if on her way home from the doctor's office she had stumbled and face-planted on the asphalt, right into a muddy puddle, maybe then she'd understand or remotely believe what she's seeing. But when she touches her face and runs her fingers through her hair, what she feels doesn't sync with the visual.

She widens both of her eyes and alternates between closing and opening them, one at a time. Her distorted reflection shifts side to side as she views it from each perspective.

Opening both eyes, she confirms that, yes, they *are* both open while her reflection only peers through one.

Stepping closer to the bloody Mary in the mirror, this Mary hesitantly reaches out her right hand.

She asks, "Are you all right?"

With held breath, Mary stares at the hand extended toward her, its fingertips flattened against the glass. She releases air from her lungs.

"I am now."

She swallows and slowly raises her left hand to the mirror until the pain stops her. Her shoulder is sore from when Jack shoved her into the wall so hard her head ricocheted off it, and her face throbs like one big artery. Still, she holds her arm up halfway, willing to lift it the remaining distance.

Her unscathed reflection looks her up and down in stunned silence. Just as Mary is about to reach the reflected hand, it draws back a few inches.

Despite the recoil, something seems to register behind the other Mary's expression. Her eyes now hold a knowing look. But her voice is tentative when she ventures, "Fool me once, shame on him."

Licking the corner of her split lip, Mary nods. "Fool me twice…"

Her reflection further retracts its outstretched hand. "Shame on me?"

"Not you," Mary says softly.

The other Mary furrows her brow. "Well…not you either." Flattening her hand to her breastbone, she shakes her head and says in a smaller voice, "Still. It *could* have been me. So easily."

"But it wasn't."

She sucks in a breath and then, with a tremor in her lips, says, "If I'd accepted that drink, maybe taken that train…"

Mary shrugs and winces at the recurring ache in her shoulder. "But you didn't."

"But I could've, almost would have, and it would've made all the difference, wouldn't it? Didn't it. For you, I mean."

"Doesn't mean you would've deserved it. That I did."

"I know." Her mirrored self nods and bites her lower lip. "But I can't believe I even agreed to meet him at the café, then actually went there. Kidding myself that it was only coffee, as if it could *only* be anything where that guy goes. He's bad for us, Mary. And he won't be the only one out there. It wasn't our fault, none of it, but we still have to…we have to know we deserve better. We have to know." She appears to draw in a number of shallow breaths. "You survived, though. You did that. You."

Swallowing, Mary nods.

"I'm proud of you."

"Proud of us."

"Us." The eyes in the mirror pan down from Mary's bloody face to her torso. "Even so. I'm so sorry."

Digging her chin into her chest, Mary looks down, too, and spies—with her good eye—the large brown stain soaked into her T-shirt.

"It's okay," she says as she tugs the wet cotton away from her skin. "It's only coffee."

Mary and Mary look up at each other and can't help but crack a smile at their very un-funny inside joke. With opposite hands, they reach for the mirror and press their palms together.

Leaning on each other, they hold each other up.

"Bloody Hell, Mary!" was originally written in 2013 in response to a webzine's call for submission: a feminist retelling of an urban legend. Its first incarnation wasn't accepted ('tis all part of the journey), but I've since unearthed and expanded on it, and this is its first publication.

Part II

Mother

Four Somethings & a Sixpence

A love story.

Something Old

She steals a glance at me from the water-welled corners of those jade eyes. She ought to be concentrating on the priest's instructions. I mean, this day certainly isn't about *me*, after all…

But she never could focus on any one person as they spoke for very long. "I'm visual, not auditory," she'd say with her usual, acute self-awareness. Now they'd call it ADD, but I used to call her "my little bundle of neuroses." I never fully bought that her short attention span had anything to do with how she best processed her information; I could damn well see the five hamsters running on the wheels of her mind in different directions, but all running *from* the same direction of her, the epicenter of her own introspective universe.

She holds the look for longer than I would have expected, considering she met my eye directly. I wish she would pay less attention to me and more on what we're supposed to. But then again, neither am I.

It's only rehearsal, but I'm standing here at the altar steps, already trying to picture her in the white gown, the veil, painted up and polished like a store mannequin that looks vaguely like someone I knew once.

Don't get me wrong; I know she'll look beautiful. Christ, she'll be breathtaking. But it won't be like what they always say about brides, that their wedding day is when they're at their prettiest. No way. She's prettiest when she's most natural. That's her way. And I'm guessing it won't be any different in marriage—she'll take at least one weekend day to marinate in her own juices, sitting around in the sweatpants she slept in and not so much as changing her crusted panties. She'll get ripe, that's for sure; that'll never change. But, just as certainly, she'll never repel. When she otherwise confines herself in manners and grace, I swear those weekend days release her soul through those oily pores. She may make the effort to look the part for the outside world—refined, poised, clean. But indoors, she's a primal one. No question about that.

At least she was, when I could be privy to her privates. Getting used to going without that for a while hasn't been the hard part, though. Not even close. Which is fine, it's not the most important thing, blah-blah-blah… My grown-up self does finally get that. I'd be lying as a man, though, if I didn't admit there are times I would give anything to feel her skin against mine, to share that again with each other. I wonder if after this whole circus of a day, she'll even be giving of herself on the wedding night.

Sex with her started out clumsy—but soft—those years ago, then became soft yet skillful, then became an outright ravaging as she bit and sucked with an insatiable fervor that finally matched my own.

God, she got me in those days. I mean *got* me, to where I never even questioned that we'd end up getting married and skip along this pathway, soulmates for life. College kids, thinking we had a clue what love and commitment were. As if either of us has a clue now.

Well, she might. She might very well. I look at her now as she finally does appear to listen to the priest, arching her back, trying too hard to look like she falls naturally into that elegant posture. Her spaghetti-strapped dress gives away that her shoulder blades keep readjusting, the muscles beneath that fresh spray-tan alternating between tensing and relaxing. My bet is tomorrow's gown is going to give it away, too, though I guess the veil will hide it. My little faker.

What she's not faking are those tears, though. Amazingly, she hasn't allowed even one to fall yet, with the command of a grade-school teacher organizing her students at the door before recess. What I've never been able to interpret with tears, though, is whether they're the happy ones or the sad ones. They always look sad, in my opinion. And if it were up to me, I'd say her expression right now looks fucking *tragic*, but her mouth is trembling between a pout and a smile. Only she could somehow do both at once.

But I'm apparently the only one who could never tell the difference, so it was therefore always my fault. I'm the one who didn't understand, *couldn't* understand, so she glided ahead of me and my endless flaws, and I had to run until I could've choked up a lung to catch up. Can't say I ever did.

As she dances the choreography, passing the phantom bouquet to her sister — the Maid of Honor — then walking around toward the Virgin Mary statue, I watch her affecting that same arrogance of a house cat with her careful, measured steps.

That little bitch.

I could hate her. I really could, and I think I do. Right now.

I've been the victim of how her warm passion can spark into violent flame from a fiery temperament that stabs with forked tongue; that is, if it isn't as easily extinguished by that cold shoulder when her heart ices over and closes you out. When she does speak, she can snatch your words and twist and stretch and snap them until you don't even know what your name is anymore. She's independent to a fault, and way too insistent on that to be a real team player in any relationship.

And yet she said yes. She was proposed to, and she said yes. She who haughtily scoffed at convention has managed to find a new outlet through her inner Bridezilla.

Which is coming to the forefront now. Man, she *really* doesn't want anything screwed up—she's kneeling before Mary now when she doesn't have to.

"I just want to be sure I get the timing right tomorrow," she tells the priest, and he's letting her. Don't we all just give her her way.

With her eyes locked on the statue, she sinks to one knee, then the other, apparently not caring whether she scuffs the toes of her pumps or crinkles the hem of her pale dress. Posture perfect, she intersects her fingers and bows her head with eyelids dropped.

From my vantage, I see her in profile. I knew she wouldn't be able to hold her spine straight for long, but I didn't expect it to slump the way it just has, as if all the air's evacuated her lungs, emptied her of her stuffing. But even from a few yards away, I can tell she's breathing—her chest heaves, and her lips, quivering at their corners, move silently as she recites the Hail Mary under her breath. When her head rises with a sniff, her cheek catches the light, and I see from the glint that she's finally releasing those tears. Class dismissed.

As she goes into what I'm guessing by now is at least her third round of prayer, I notice for the first time the *quiet*. I look away from her to scan the bridal party standing up here, the parents and readers sitting down there, and they're all stone still, just watching her. I feel a pressure weighing on my breastbone as I gaze back at her there, all by herself, slouched in humble supplication to her Catholic goddess.

The good thing about these rehearsals, I'm realizing, is not just being fed our lines and following the numbered dance steps on the floor. It's not the physical preparation, it's the mental, the emotional. It's so we can finally stare this situation down for what it is, what it will be. Confront the ghost, and try to give it peace.

She's never looked lonelier. Or smaller. She's got the delicate bones of a little girl who's fallen on the playground and sits scared and crying quietly for help.

It's the vulnerability I saw when we first met, first fell in love. It's what made me love her, actually, and why I still do, even when she tries too hard to protect it under that useless bulletproof shell.

I see the girl again who lay there with her chocolate-brown locks tangled all over her face, the air squeaking out her allergy-congested nostrils, and the drool already dried white against the dark pillowcase. The girl who'd wake up with a snort and laugh at herself because she'd heard it, too. The girl who'd then twist herself around in my sheets and curl into me for another cozy few minutes of snoozing, her breath tickling my chest hair as I reached to stroke her peach-fuzzed cheek and cup her shoulder to fold her closer to me. That's who she is.

That's my girl.

"Sir?"

"Hey, buddy, he's talking to you, man."

"Huh? Oh, sorry, sorry," I mutter. I didn't realize it was my turn now.

Even though she's still kneeling over there, it appears the priest's reverence for prayer is taking a back seat to his agenda for this production. This church really cranks out the weddings, and the next bridal party is already filing into the back pews to wait.

In the meantime, then, he's trying to salvage the time she's using up by checking on the rest of us. He's addressing each of us in turn to recap our major roles, since we'll surely be booted out as soon as the rest of this faux ceremony is done. Godspeed!

"You, Best Man?" the priest asks again.

"Yep, man. That's me," I answer.

"You remember, now, that you're the one bringing their rings?"

"I do."

Something New

The poor thing. I'm watching her smile and laugh, just carrying on frivolous conversation at the rehearsal-dinner table, keeping everyone distracted from the fact that she's cutting her food and moving it around on the plate, but not eating it. She's already telling everyone she won't be long for the night, and she nervously guzzles down her water "to stay hydrated and look fresh in the morning." And apparently the reason she was absent so long after we first got here was because she needed to check her voicemail, in case anything came up at work while she was out today.

Uh-huh. I know what's up, but what's a sister to do other than honor her kid sister's request? Smile along with the program, that's what. Take the bouquet tomorrow when it's handed to me and straighten out the train after she's walked, just like she did for me. Contrary to what people have been labeling me all night, it's really *Matron* of Honor. Gawd, that makes me sound so old.

When I was married, I was much younger than she is now, more naïve and far less analytical. And I certainly didn't give a second thought to the pressures that are part and parcel of reality but that twenty-somethings never think could happen to them. Thirty-somethings like her, though — they start thinking about it.

At that age, you start to feel how hangovers take a matter of days, not hours, to recover from. How the skin that used to be the bane of your existence when it boiled over in greasy pimples now can't suck up enough of that moisturizer you scrub into it twice daily to keep it from creasing. How even the fittest of us can't prevent the appearance of cellulite, and how the bushy eyebrows that once embarrassed you are now thinning at such a rate you can see yourself penciling them in in the foreseeable future. How the coarse grey hairs have infiltrated the front of your hairline, and how one day you might not only find them on your *head*.

It's only a matter of time when our bodies stop keeping up and start to betray us. It's a time when mortality becomes more confrontational as you stare it in the face each morning in the bathroom mirror and discover changes in mass as you lather in the shower.

When she should just be celebrating her yet-youthfulness and making the most of her life as it is right now, she's obsessing. I can see it, and I think others might have, too, at the rehearsal. I don't blame her—I'm obsessing, too, and could only assume at least one of us would have to break at some point. I don't think that was the full-on emotional crash we're both expecting, but it was at least a fissure letting out some steam. Which is good. I'd be more concerned if she didn't let it out at all, especially under the ordinary stress that comes with a wedding anyway—all that planning, the decisions, the appointments, the coordination of all the different vendors, and all on top of a full-time job…a job that is loved, a *life* that is loved, but might now be in jeopardy.

It's more than the typical adjustment that marriage already entails, and I just wish that she would tell him. He has a right to know what he's possibly getting into, even if she doesn't feel he has any power to do anything about it.

It all came out in the open to *me*, anyway, during her final fitting at the bridal boutique. She'd asked last-minute if I minded driving over to give her a quick, objective opinion since I live closer by than our mother. Plus, it would make sense for me to learn how to do up the bustle and all that fun Matron of Honor stuff.

Of course I would agree! This is my baby sister, who I used to dress up like she was my doll—and who never fussed when I put her in our eldest brother's hand-me-downs so I could use *her* to date my Barbie in the absence of a Ken. The little girl who listened wide-eyed at the colorful, gruesomely descriptive bedtime stories I made up for her, overlooking the fact that their purpose was to help her sleep. The one who squealed and splashed at me in her baby pool, where we would dance and compose spontaneous songs together. The girl that I couldn't have run toward fast enough when I heard her cries of shock and pain on the playground.

So, there I found myself clapping from the shop's velvety wingback chair as I watched my living doll rotate on the pedestal, looking like the chicest of brunette Barbies. Perfectly natural that she'd want me there to share in this.

It was after the seamstress had zipped and buttoned her up, then left us to critique between ourselves, that my sister started speaking up — first, to giggle at the vanity of the situation as she stood elevated one foot off the ground and encased in mirrors.

"It's good to see from all angles, though, that it covers up my worst bits."

Within seconds of finishing that sentence, I saw her go pale and purse her lips together. Her back was to me, but her reflection met my eyes, and I just then noticed how darkened the circles beneath hers were.

Right, okay. This day wasn't just about the dress but what was — well, could be — residing beneath it and growing under my kid sister's skin.

She had turned around and stepped off her stage to crouch at my knees and inform me gently of her discovery. She hadn't been to the doctor yet to know for sure, but if there was still hope in this, it certainly wasn't carried by her whispers. It turns out she'd consulted the internet and arrived at an amateur diagnosis for what she tangibly felt. As her glassy eyes brimmed, I affectionately pinched her chin between my thumb and index finger.

"Hey, sissy. It's going to be okay. Time will tell exactly what's going on, but it's gonna be all right." After a pause, I felt compelled to continue with "But, I think you should see about this sooner rather than later."

She said she would consider it but was leaning toward blissful ignorance. The show must go on — as planned and with no script changes that new knowledge might bring. She might inwardly fear for her own life crashing to a halt, but what lumps the audience couldn't see wouldn't kill them, at least.

"Hey, it's not going to kill *you* either. You need to believe that. And he should know," I said, after my more sanguine encouragements failed.

"Not yet. Not if there still might be nothing for him to know," she stubbornly replied, though her face gave away that her pessimism and flair for the dramatic didn't really hold on to that least bit of faith.

I'll have to summon the faith and strength of two, then, and weave it into a protective cocoon to enfold her, see her through this. And if she is still pricked through that, I will bleed alongside her.

And so I sit here, dabbing my lips with crisp white linen, staring at the crimson stain they leave and trying to muster more of an appetite than she has. Wondering if, after all, she might by now know something that she hasn't told me.

Something Borrowed

I wore them, my baby girl wore them, and now my baby's baby girl is wearing them.

Looking on from my plane of existence, if I still physically had eyes, they'd be shedding tears at the sight of Mother dressing Grown Daughter in her bridal gown. My strand of pearls is providing the pièce de résistance to the entire ensemble, if I may say so myself. That they've yellowed over the years is trivial; they only match the champagne tone of her silk dupioni all the more.

I would have never thought I'd have a prayer — had I been a praying woman in life, that is — of viewing this moment, of sharing in it somehow, being as sickly as I was when my granddaughter was just a little girl. Though my bones weren't nearly old enough, I could feel in their marrow that my days were drawing to a close. This knowing brought me a sense of peace, at least, that I could recline into for the rest of my time on earth.

My, my…it could be split seconds ago when I was dressing my own daughter, though Time for me now follows no such unit of measurement. It merely stretches into an infinite space that I can now fully see and comprehend, even if they cannot yet. Someday, they will also see how it expands to fold in upon itself, such that my granddaughter's wedding day could be yesterday whereas my own marital vows might be uttered tomorrow.

But even as I look forward to my wedding day, I can look back on it now with a warm heart that would still skip a beat—if it still beat at all—at the sight of my beloved. My, was he a pleasant vision...

Oh, he's with me now, of course. Just as we had often suspected in life, our souls are interlaced, beginning where the other ends and in all other ways fulfilling those sentimental sweet nothings that young lovers will coo to one another. If we still had faces, I'd have loved to have seen the expression on his when he discovered that we really would be stuck together for good! (Ah, it is a true grace that his jovial, undulating guffaw is one keepsake he got to bring with him to forever please me—I can hear it now as he chuckles at my teasing.)

At any rate, I know he likes to listen to me compliment him, so, as I was saying...my, was he a pleasant vision. Hair like waves of coffee that I'd drink with my eyes each morning for a buzz that would last all day. Eyes like emeralds that made me a rich woman for life. A smile of white teeth that dazzled me beyond the new string of freshwater pearls adorning my neck that he had given me as a wedding gift.

When I saw all this at the end of that aisle extending before me, and really processed that all this was standing there waiting for *me*, it took my breath away. He in his ivory waistcoat, I in unembellished ivory satin, with a cascade of pale chrysanthemums picked from my mother's garden... He holding me closely, swaying me round and round as he hummed "All the Things You Are" in my ear long after the band had stopped and the guests had left... This was a day that stayed with me until my last breath really did expel into the atmosphere for the rest of eternity.

We had a good life. It was a hard, selfless, sparing one through those early times of war, but a happy one so long as we fought in the same trenches during our personal battles, as all marriages must trudge through one time or another. In some way, there was an innocence maintained in those days even when our eyes were wide open. Perhaps it's easier for me to say this perched here at this vantage, where anything perceived in retrospect can be seen in advance—not having to learn the hard way. But even in life, and at even younger than her age, I feel our foresight was closer to twenty-twenty than that of this generation that squints to blur out what they don't wish to see.

And the thinning gold hook sliding into its clasp at the back of my granddaughter's neck isn't all that I can see now. My vision can penetrate those emotional layers she fortifies herself within, as well as the biological ones, so she can't conceal anything from *me*.

There was a time I'd taken her and her sister to the playground, in which there was a moment spanning the length of two to three seconds that I could not for the rest of my days forgive myself for. She was four and in pigtails—I had brushed and brushed those silken tresses with such care that morning and tied them up for her. She had looked so gosh darn pretty, too, as pretty as now. But I'd looked away to find the source of a different child's scream, just to hear her own not a second later.

I like to think that I can puncture through this dimensional membrane that now divides us, as I'm hoping to do right now, just to tell her what I've already told her all the days stretching behind and ahead of her in one continuous strand:

"My darling girl, please know there is never a heartbeat of yours that ticks by when I am not watching you. If I can't lift those troubles that weigh at your breast, I will at least be here, watching, always watching, seeing you through the crosses you must bear. Never alone, never unloved. Even from afar, I reside within you. And we'll be together again in but a blink."

Something Blue

It comes with the job. It's not my favorite part a' the day, but it isn't the worst, and usually people are only here for a night or two, so they don't make that much trash.

Interesting what you find, though, some a' the time. Empty wrappers and bottles from the mini bar, plane tickets, price tags come off new clothes for a night on the town, loads of wads of snotty Kleenex. Yeah, you know, so a little bit a' everything. It's not like I dig through the stuff. The trash bags are clear, and, anyways, sometimes it helps pass the time to just make a game of it. Like kids when they play "I Spy" on the playground, but solo.

"I spy a used condom."

"I spy a button and tube a' ChapStick."

"I spy a plastic tampon applicator and disposable razor."

This morning I step into my next room, and it's such a wreck, I actually have ta look around to make sure that, yeah, this is the bridal suite.

It's humid from the shower she couldn'ta taken too long ago, and the wet air is thick with deodorant and perfume. There's a garment bag from some fancy-lookin' bridal store flopped over the back of the chair still and a bathrobe twisted on the bed, with matching terrycloth slippers kicked halfway under the bed frame. There are pink paper plates filled with crumbs and half-eaten coffee cakes shoved against the stems a' plastic, partially drunk champagne flutes. Balls and shreds a' gold foil lyin' around from the champagne bottle, and God knows where the cork landed. Wasted bottles a' water with maybe two sips taken out are sittin' on every flat surface, along with compacts and eye-shadow applicators. On the ottoman is an empty shoebox slanted all topsy-turvy on its lid with tissue paper flyin' out, and a couple of those silicone packets stuffed in there for freshness fell out onto the floor special for me to pick up. On the desk in front a' the mirror, hairpins and flower petals are scattered around, and strands of hair are caught on some of 'em. It's a right mess for a lady and her attendants to've made, but what can ya do. It's her wedding day.

Right about now, they're probably on their way to the church or already starting the ceremony or whatever. Sometimes, I get curious about the guests' lives, and pretendin' about what they're like is another way I pass the time. But otherwise, it's business as usual, and I just wanna get done what needs ta get done so I can move on.

I straighten or sidestep their piles as necessary; I never want to be accused of messin' with anyone's stuff. Rehang the bath-robe and swap the wet towels for dry. Tuck in the bedsheets and straighten the cover. Replenish the toiletries, and, if I'm in a good mood and feelin' *really* generous, I'll leave extra samples of the shampoo and conditioner, maybe an extra chocolate-mint square or two on the pillow.

I don't really give a rat's ass for these people, how much they pay ta sleep here and how much they think that entitles 'em to, but I can still get curious. I like the messy rooms, actually, 'cause it reminds me no one's perfect, and ain't that the truth.

I'm thinkin' about this little pearl a' wisdom as I move on from the bed to the bathroom to start emptyin' all the wastebas-kets. Mostly yellow tissue again, heaps this time—probably a little drama queen on our hands, unable to believe it's true that today pretty little her gets to be the precious little princess she's always dreamed of. *Gag*.

Not an interesting game for me to play this time with all this Kleenex stuffed in here. I jostle the contents around a little as I jerk up the bag to remove it from the basket, but before I tie it in a knot, I see there's somethin' else in there after all. I knit my eyebrows and stick out my lower lip in tryin' to make it out. I can only see part of it, so, surprising myself with how nosy I can be, I give an extra little shake to dislodge a lipstick-stained tissue wad from on top of it.

Huh.

"I spy a pregnancy test."

I never used one a' these myself—was pretty much a given each time I got laid I'd pop out a kid—but I know from TV what these little white sticks are and what that little blue indicator means.

Before I push my cart out into the hallway and let the heavy door swing shut behind me, I throw a couple of extra shampoos on the counter and five chocolate-mint squares on 'er pillow.

And a Silver Sixpence in Her Shoe

One. The daily countdown is over, and it's déjà-vu all over again, watching her there kneeling in front of Mary. It isn't as eerily quiet this time, although this a cappella rendition gives the singer's "Ave Maria" a haunting quality. It echoes through the cathedral and seems to cast a foggy mist over the bride herself; her spirit pulsates behind the filmy haze. My ghost.

If she's agitated, she's hiding it expertly behind her veil, that crazy-long veil that dragged the floor several feet behind when her dad escorted her to the altar. In spite of myself, I felt that uncomfortable knot in my throat at the sight of him giving her away. I know him to be a mild, quiet man of few words, but, man, did that expression in his eyes in a split second gush out pages of a family's history. He's not seeing what everyone else is; he's seeing the eight-year-old that I often see, even though I didn't even know her then. God, was that a fucking beautiful moment.

So, now I need to own up that what I'm seeing now is not some paranormal aura surrounding her—it's moisture in my eyes, for the second fucking time this morning.

Fuck. I thought rehearsal would've made this easier. Practice makes perfect and all that. And I got through my cameo smoothly, didn't fuck up and forget the rings or anything.

Christ, though. It's never going to get easier, is it?

I haven't even written out their wedding card. Or bought it yet, for that matter. Who am I supposed to write the check out to anyway? "Mr. and *Mrs.*"? "My Best Buddy and The One That Got Away"?

Fuck. Get it together. Just be happy for them.

Heaving as deep a breath as my cigarette-punished lungs can fill, I force myself to level my gaze at my little ghost bride.

Baby, I think the best gift I can give to you is to leave you two alone. Be a man, step aside, and when this production is over, exit stage left.

But when I see her crying again like this, I know that's something I could never do. I need to stay here, be here. I owe them both that much. And there's something different that her posture is saying this time. Less fragile and more…resolved. She always did have so much to teach me; her lessons might've been rants at my expense, but her intentions were right. And she's teaching me something now…a lesson in, I don't know. Grace.

Two times now I've had to pull the Kleenex out of my strapless bra. Such a sentimental schmuck. But, oh…

Oh, sissy, you're prettier than all the dolls I ever had or now buy for my daughter.

My sister never had dolls because she thought they were creepy, so she accumulated stuffed animals instead. I swear I can see them all piled around her still, just like she'd bury herself in them after I tucked her in bed. She'd have at least a dozen, but she'd outstretch her thin little arms to make sure she was hugging them all.

She never *had* been one to leave anyone out, so I'm sure it must be killing her to keep what she is from so many that she loves. I'm grateful she told me from the get-go, though, so I could be here and inspect her for any signs of breaking. And if she hadn't told me, and I found this out after anyone else, I'd have kicked her sweet behind.

She's had her reservations, to say the least, and I'd be lying if I said I didn't understand. My oldest wasn't planned either, and it freaked the hell out of me. Sure, I can't forget feeling that way. But I was freaked out for different reasons — mainly, I didn't want to break it! What a surreal feeling to come home with this extra person who didn't exist before and take on the responsibility of making sure it didn't die. But I was also younger than she is, and I suppose in a different mindset. I was never happy in my career, and, at the risk of setting my gender back decades, I really did just always want to be a mom.

And as I told *her*, there's no shame in that. But I offered to be her daycare if she wants to go back to full-time work after her leave. It's at least something we can be open to talking about if the need arises.

Yet there might not even be a pregnancy, and, well, she's always been a pretty liberal Catholic (how's that for an oxymoron if I've ever heard one) when it comes to women's choice...

But I do understand the alternative to that could mean bidding farewell — at least for a while — to their life as they know it. Their travels, ambitions... They move in a worldly circle and haven't really given much thought to saving for the future, what with still paying rent on an overpriced, undersized urban apartment and needing the second bedroom just to store her wardrobe. But contrary to her terrors, she's more maternal than she realizes. Personally, I think she'll take to it absurdly well. She'll surprise herself.

If the need arises.

Three times the charm! Three times that pearl necklace has walked down the aisle, three times it has accessorized those vows, and, for the third time, it looks like this one will be a keeper!

As I've said before, I wasn't a praying woman, but I was always a sucker for a place of worship, be it a cathedral or a mosque. It's no matter, really. Of course, it's easy for me to know from where I exist, but I think if the living spent less time debating the differences between religions, the more they would discover the similarities. It doesn't matter who is called what; an egg is still an egg no matter how you fry it. It's the leaps of faith that matter and following a common sense of regard and decency in how you live your life and allow it to touch others.

That's the reason why I didn't mind bringing our children up Catholic; I knew it was important to my husband, and I assumed it would, in the absence of any pressuring on our parts, assist the kids in making an educated decision for themselves when they came of age. As the dice fell, it resulted in a fairly even split, but a peaceful one, with no one imposing their belief systems on another. To each their own. Certainly, I had the occasional theological debate with my spouse, but we remained amicable about it, even when we had to respectfully agree to simply disagree. And as he and I can now witness firsthand, it turns out we were both right!

I never did miss a wedding or a Sunday mass, though — except, of course, for when the children were little and I stayed home with them. We attended a simple church, a rural one, surely nothing as stupendous as this city structure. Still, it had lovely pockets of fragmented and multihued glass that shone like a prism when pierced with sunbeams. It was as though every color held a key to your ultimate destiny, shreds of disparate fortunes that would all add up to an overall happy life. They were very simply constructed, especially as compared to these exquisite panes depicting centuries-old stories in the finest of detail; yet, in the simplicity, one could see oneself. There wasn't another face or symbol to distract from the Truth of one's own essence, and in that, those basic little windows awarded us immortality. At least for the time being.

As I take in these wondrous beams vividly inscribed in braided Celtic patterns, my thoughts recall the rotted, splintering rafters of our little farmers' place of worship. I do not doubt now that the building was violating two and twenty safety codes by modern-day standards, but its musty fragility is what held a sort of enchantment over me in those days. It illustrated for me even then the temporal quality of an earthbound life, how even the structures that survive us may yet one day crumble into the sea.

"With that finite nature in mind, regardless of the everlasting life you may look forward to hereafter, I wish this for you, Dear Granddaughter: that you not take *this* life for granted. That you not take the lives beside and within you for granted either. These are the building blocks with which you will raise yourself to the skies."

Four condoms. I spy *four* condoms in just this one wastebasket! Holy hell, somebody has no problem gettin' the wind back in his sails…

Five hours ago, I was first getting out of bed for the day and was still an unmarried man.

Five days ago, I was still nursing the hangover of the prior weekend's bachelor party, and, man, was it the worst I've had since those St. Patty's Days in college when we'd blow off class all day for the bars and wake up with green tongues.

Five weeks ago, we were attending our weekend Pre-Cana class, filling out our workbooks and verifying what we already knew on where the other stood as far as finances, children, etc., getting that all out of the way so we could eavesdrop on — and laugh at — other couples bickering over these same issues apparently for the first time.

Five months ago, we were scanning china settings and stainless-steel pots for our registry, deciding on bath towels and invitation fonts, and talking about how we didn't understand why people always say marriage changes everything.

Five years ago, we had just started dating after years of friendship. It was the taboo pairing that was never to be — we both individually honored our, er, mutual friend too much to cross hurtful boundaries. Little did we know at the time that we were both thinking this way…well, *feeling* this way. I don't know if that would have made a difference, at least those years ago. I mean, we share standards of, you know, social etiquette, so we probably would've continued denying ourselves even if we'd known our interest in the other was reciprocated. I'm not the guy who steals his best friend's girl.

But I did, I guess. Well, I don't think *steal* is the right word. It's hard to explain what happened to make the earth shift in a certain way and somehow make the situation of her and me crossing the platonic line perfectly acceptable. Maybe it was my buddy moving on to plenty of women after her. Maybe it was because some unknown statute of limitation in years had passed us by, and it really was cosmically okay to do.

Or maybe there is no excuse to lamely fall back on. Maybe it's simply because I had fallen in love with her.

I'm not going to be the asshole who hides behind the cliché "All's fair in love and war." My buddy was a casualty, and that's *not* cool with me. I'm not going to pretend to defend myself. All I could do at the time was hope that he would eventually understand. If he found love himself—instead of this endless game he plays with women, as if he's daring himself *not* to love—he would have to understand. And if not, as much as it hurt, I guess I'd already made my choice between the two, hadn't I.

Believe me, I know what a lucky son of a bitch I am.

First of all, I got the girl. My girl. And whatever risks we took to make this happen have been worth it. Watching her over there as she prays, looking like a little girl on her First Communion, I couldn't question that for an instant now.

Second of all, I've got the best buddy on the planet to have let me get the girl, and be cool enough about it to stand by my side in support today.

Third of all, and most certainly last but not least…(guess I *am* doling out the clichés today after all. What can I say, I'm really excited and nervous right now and can barely think or speak clearly…shit, I'm glad I even made it through my vows). Anyway, as I was saying, or thinking, or at least trying to articulate into a thought, because she just told me this morning, and it hasn't had much time to register, and I still can't believe it…

Well, third of all, my girl is carrying my baby.

Six. Six times I've recited the Hail Mary, and I'm going in for the seventh. I was only supposed to do three, had only practiced with three, but I'm doing seven. At least. This is ridiculous, but I just feel rooted right on this spot, and it seems the singer has picked up on my cue to carry on an extra verse or two. Or three.

I can't explain this. I'm kneeling here in the same precise spot I was last night, and I know there's this freaking congregation of people behind me watching, all watching, but I somehow still feel alone. Not lonely, not isolated, but peacefully secluded. Does that make sense? Does anything anymore?

Though my head is bowed, I sneak my eyes upward to stroke the contours of Her face and pause at Her mildly smiling lips that seemed to smirk more last night. Dropping my gaze downward, I visually trek the terrain within the carved folds of Her tunic and veil, which flow into those of the cloth swaddling Her infant. I dwell on the wee ivory limbs, the tiny finger that extends out as though to anoint me, whereas last night I thought it meant to accuse.

Six years ago, I did not remotely feel the need to get married, ever. I was so content with my life, with my career, my social life.

It wasn't that I was anti-marriage or anything; I'd simply realized that if marriage and having a family wasn't in the cards for me, I'd be content. I had already been through enough relationships to know they were never easy, and I didn't delude myself that even being with the ever-elusive "One" would be a walk in the park. Commitment is work, and there's no way around that basic, painfully obvious fact. If I was ever going to get married, man, did that guy need to be worth it.

I told all of this to my fiancé—oh my God, no, my *husband* now! Okay, so I told this to my *husband* on our second date already. I figured that would give him fair warning of what he was getting into. I know I can be a feisty one, and until him, not one single guy had given me up to three strikes before I was out. Unless I broke up with him first.

Six months ago, I had an awkward encounter with an ex.

Okay, he's not really just "an ex"…he was my first love. Sure, I'd dated guys before him, but he was the first I ever really loved. We lasted for a while, too, making it to that infamous make-or-break point of around two years, but, unfortunately—and as I'm sure you've guessed—it yielded the latter. Yeah, I was the one to do it, but I'll admit to this day that it hurt like hell. I lost my best friend that day, and it was like the air was sucked out of my lungs. I had hoped the friendship could be preserved, though, since we had technically been friends for ten entire days before admitting our feelings in a highly inebriated state at one of our favorite college bars, proceeding to massively make out there, then on the sidewalk, then outside the door of my campus apartment. Lady that I was, I did not invite him up that night (I waited until the *third* time we massively made out at a campus bar), and, gentleman that he was, he didn't try to seduce me into procuring said invitation.

Man, he got me in those days. I mean *got* me. He was so ridiculously smart and challenged my perspectives, really made me think. He always did have so much to teach me.

I guess I'd get carried away and think I was challenging him in kind when, really, I just scapegoated him for whatever else might have bothered me that day. It satisfied me to tear him in shreds, feel that I out-argued the argumentative, even though I knew I was hitting below the belt almost every time. It got to the point where I became conscious of just wanting to make him hurt, just wanting to belittle him into submission, for whatever satisfaction was in that. He toughed it out, though. He did it for me. But I just couldn't do it to him anymore.

Because I loved him, I broke up with him.

Okay, I really don't know how many more verses of "Ave Maria" the singer can repeat to help me out here. I breathe in steadily and raise my chin to stare at Mary point-blank.

Six months ago, then, when we were all hanging out with the usual crowd—which amazingly still includes our little trio—my ex admitted what he felt. Only minutes before, I'd drunkenly decided to join the smoking crowd out on the frigid sidewalk, while my now-husband stayed inside. There were a few of us out there initially, but before I realized it, it was just us two. And after lighting a cigarette right beside his in his mouth and inserting it between my lips, he stated it quite simply. Just to put it out there, not because he expected anything to change.

Oh God, I can't keep up this praying any longer. It's time to get back on my feet.

As I lift my gown like a lady of another century to step back around to the center of the altar, I mean to look at my husband but accidentally lock eyes with him. The Best Man.

I'm the first to know that I need to work harder at checking my ego at the door, but I swear, his eyes look glassy. Surely that doesn't have anything to do with me. It couldn't have anything to do with me. But it could, couldn't it?

Shit. All these years later, and I'm still making him cry. I can't handle it.

Focus. Refocus on the one who matters now. Don't get me wrong—I really don't need reminding of who matters now. I suppose that's what my thoughts were trying to get at just when I caught the sweat beading on the priest's bald forehead and realized I had to get back on schedule.

He, the Best Man, had told me what he felt. And I, at that moment, couldn't have seen more clearly what *I* felt. We were too alike, and I'd since found my match in the man who's actually mismatched with me in some ways. A yin to a yang, if I want to be cheesy about it, but that's what works—core similarities, yes, but also enough differences to help the opposing bits fit right into each other like the pieces of a jigsaw puzzle.

Looking away, I allow the eyes in my peripheral vision to blur into obscurity, and I focus intently on those of my husband.

He momentarily clasps my hands to rub his thumbs reassuringly over them, and I think of how, six weeks ago, I was freaking out that I'd skipped my period. That I'd begun feeling fatigued and lightheaded. Admittedly, my initial alarm might've been irrational, but I know my body and make an effort to listen to it. My sister was the first person I could think of to tell any suspicions, the one person I knew wouldn't freak out or, more importantly, judge. And as it turns out, that wasn't my final bridal-gown fitting after all when, weeks later, I noticed a slight thickening at my waistline.

Six days ago, then, I started to become nauseated, but, even weirder, it felt as though my gums were softening, and I'd gained this really intense sense of smell—I could detect my manager's halitosis from across the office instead of just when he hovered piggishly over my shoulder, for instance.

Still, I stayed in denial until, about six hours prior to the rehearsal, I took a pregnancy test before my parents picked me up from our apartment to have an intimate lunch, just the three of us. My husband had already left to pick up his tuxedo, so I had an hour of privacy.

Then, six minutes into the rehearsal dinner at the hotel, I made up an excuse to sneak back to my room. (Yes, *my* room, not ours. We've already been living together for a year, but I'm still a traditional girl at heart and demanded separate rooms until tonight.) Once there, I pulled out the second test stick from the package that I'd hidden in the bowels of my biggest bag. Shit, yep, that's when I got confirmation on what the first stick had already told me.

Many tears and makeup reapplications later, I hurried myself back to dinner before anyone could suspect anything. I was just going to have to tough it out until the wedding was past. And hey, I figured, the good news was we could screw like rabbits on our honeymoon and not have to worry about getting pregnant, seeing as I already was… All right, look, I've got to find my positives where I can.

The thing is, the positives have steamrolled me in abundance, completely and unexpectedly.

First of all, my sister was nothing but encouraging at a time I believed I had everything to lose.

Second of all, my husband actually cried—tears of joy, I may add—when I broke down and padded barefoot to his hotel room at three o'clock this morning to finally tell him, just between the two of us for now.

Third of all, when I was kneeling before the statue of Mary just moments ago, the babe in Her arms, which had brought me such misery and dread last night, this time snapped everything into calming perspective and infused me with a warming wave of purpose.

I'm afraid. Hell, I'm terrified. But I'm not alone. I am loved by the people surrounding me and, my God, actually *inside* of me. People who will pick me up when I fall, just like when I was a little girl.

As the priest concludes our final blessing, I rest one hand lightly at my belly and caress my grandmother's pearls with the other, before folding them both back into my husband's. I stare directly into his eyes and feel our anxious souls connect, preparing to lock it all in with that time-honored seal in just six more seconds:

"You may now kiss the bride."

"Four Somethings & a Sixpence" was written in 2010 for the Accentuate Writers short story contest, winning First Place for "The Wedding" theme. This was my first fiction contest as an aspiring author, and the story was originally published as a standalone ebook by Vagabondage Press in 2015.

The Glass Floor

A sci-fi story.

Paris, France
22nd Century

A drop of red snuffed the torch below, breaking Emme-line's blank stare. She blinked twice, her view through the glass-bottomed elevator blurring as her veins pulsed.

Situated in back, she darted glances at those around her as she casually eased the small scarf from her breast pocket. She wiped her nose with it, then let the cream silk slip from her fingers. Bent to pick it up. With one discreet swipe, she cleared the floor of blood and stood.

Tucking the soiled cloth back into her pocket, she gazed again through the polycarbonate platform at the immense statue below, its copper flame shrinking from her ascent.

Ding.

The doors slid open, and she caught her lab scientist by the elbow on their way out.

"Seren, mind if we have a word? We'll just be a moment," she added for the Inspection Unit, which her assistant proceeded to lead to a conference room. Dropping her smile, Emmeline steered the young brunette toward an onyx wall, waving a hand to open a panel to the restroom.

Inside, she tapped her wrist directly onto a sensor to lock the door behind them. "Please," she offered, extending a hand to an open stall.

"Oh, er, Ms. Frey, I actually don't need to—"

"Please." Her hand now rigid as a blade, she gave the air a little chop.

Seren complied with a meek nod, first removing her white lab coat to hang on a hook.

Emmeline strolled into the stall beside hers. A black bowl folded down from the wall as she entered, and she perched just at the edge of its contoured seat between the foot pads, doubling over to look below the partition at the neighboring space, watchful for any sign. She heard fabric shuffle, and then Seren's toes tapped on the tile. Until, suddenly, they stopped. Tendons flexed.

In the silence, Emmeline heard Seren's breathing deepen.

"Ms. Singh," she began, steepling her fingertips together as she leaned on her knees, "may I ask if you're injured?"

"Injured? No, I—"

"Ill?"

"I—n-no. I'm fine. But thank you."

Giving herself a moment, Emmeline sighed and removed the silk square from her blazer pocket. Worrying its edges with her thumbs a few seconds, she opened it to the crimson stain and passed it underneath the stall wall.

"You leaked in the lift."

The breathing beside her turned ragged. Seren's ankles teetered above her high heels. A clear drop splashed against a pointed toe, followed by another. After a small squeak of sorts, the silk was yanked off Emmeline's palm.

"I don't think anyone saw," Emmeline said, grateful *she* had seen before the lady could sit on that white coat.

Beyond her door, a faucet dripped, tapping down the seconds for her to rally more courage. She rubbed her flattened palms back and forth, lowering her volume. "Do you…have what you need?"

No response.

Emmeline ran her damp hands along her thighs.

Another still moment passed.

Then, "Am I…sacked?"

"No." Emmeline said it more forcefully than she'd wanted, almost angrily, so she softened her tone when she asked, "Do you have any supply?"

A phlegm-filled sniff then cough.

The faucet kept thrumming its countdown. No more time.

"Seren, *do* you?"

"Not much," she finally answered. "I-I've needed to ration."

"You need a fix for today?"

A jagged sigh, then whisper. "Yes."

"Okay," Emmeline said. "Keep the scarf for backup, and…"

"Backup? To what? I don't—"

"Just…give me a moment."

Emmeline raised her eyes to the ceiling and stood before she could change her mind, lowering her trousers to the floor and poising in a slight squat to spread her thighs. Plucked a condom from between them. Breaking the prophylactic open, she pinched the cotton string of a single, unused tampon and held it beneath the partition. It dangled as she trembled.

"Oh my Gaia," Seren whispered, snatching it straight away. "Thank you."

"Ms. Singh," Emmeline pushed out her throat to smooth a shaking voice, "I don't need to tell you your discretion is vital."

"N-no. I understand."

Do you? Refastening her trousers, Emmeline licked her lower lip. A putrid pocket of unease bubbled up from her gut. She hadn't thought this through, not any of it. Yet could she regret it? She wouldn't.

Muffled beside her, she heard, "I'm so sorry about this, Ms. Frey."

Fingers latched to her lips, Emmeline swayed from the waist. She closed her eyes and drew a deep inhale. "Enough now. Inspector's waiting."

Sun streamed through the meeting room's broad panes, which the executive assistant adjusted to a darker shade by twisting his wrist anticlockwise. Madame Inspector grinned tightly at him from across the conference table.

"No, thank you, young man," she said when he offered her refreshments. "Gentlewomen?" She looked around at the rest of her team.

He smiled as he served the ladies' individual requests. Deep creases lined his forehead beneath a greying, thinning widow's peak, and she spied the slim band on his finger.

"Tell me, Monsieur," she began, "have you and your wife any children of your own?"

Pausing mid-pour, he straightened and ran a hand down his abdomen. "Four," he said with a proud glint in his eye.

"Four," she repeated with gusto. "Not all through FerLiberté?"

"Oh, yes."

"Marvelous. And have you worked here very long?"

"Only a few months. Just temping 'til Ms. Frey's regular assistant returns from paternity leave. He's taking the year."

"You enjoy temping?"

"Very much. More time at home with the kids."

"Good of you. And your wife?"

"Fund manager. Full time."

"So she's…"

"Reaped and ridded, absolutely. Didn't want to chance anything."

"Indeed. Well, you look great for four. I hope there haven't been complications."

"Not with FerLiberté, Madame Inspector."

"Marvelous," she said, just as Mesdames Frey and Singh rejoined them, faces flushed yet smiling. If a little too widely. Singh blinked too quickly as well, and Frey looked ruddy as her auburn hair.

Their abrupt separation from the group would go unquestioned but not unnoticed. Not any more than Ms. Frey's widening yet admirably hidden waistline, which of course couldn't be inquired into when a woman's weight and measurements were her legal right to withhold. Productivity hadn't diminished to any perceptible degree, which lessened any grounds for concern. And what could be more trivial than a silk pocket square that had been there minutes before but now was not.

Still, Madame Inspector would go on unquestioning but not unnoticing. The Directors did so like a thorough report.

A holographic *19:28* glowed above the desk surface. Emmeline stared at the clock, then glanced up to see Seren approach from the hall. Her temporary assistant gone for the evening, she tapped a spot on her desk twice so the transparent door to her headspace would slide open.

Emmeline strained to smile as the scientist entered the room. "Well done today. None of us expected the inspection this early."

"Hopefully we pass muster."

"We always do."

"Sorry to bother you at day's end, but I wanted to thank—"

Emmeline raised a finger, and Seren simply clasped her hands behind her back.

Walking up to a clear wall overlooking the atrium, Emmeline contemplated the statue below, the glass elevator lifting and lowering just behind it. A grand sculpture, though a miniature, gifted to France centuries ago by the then "United States" — now split among superpowers — in return for the colossus still standing in its Newer Delhi Harbour. The fair lady had been saved from the Seine, before the rising river that flooded the Île aux Cygnes could wet her robes as well.

Madame la Présidente was only too happy to lend her as FerLiberté International's figurehead. For preservation, certainly, but also as a token of gratitude for FerLiberté's contribution to women's rights, appreciated and utilized by much of the parliament's female majority. It was with no small amount of cheek, too, that France should crown one of Britain's organizations with a symbol of its rejected sovereignty — especially given the UK's ongoing "Breturn" to the Continent as it lost coastline (and its capital) to the sea. Brits had skittered and scattered all over Europe, much of FerLiberté's staff among them.

The window fogged in front of Emmeline's face as she heaved a single yet determined exhale out her nose. Snapping her hand up again, she pressed her palm downward to shroud the walls in opaque beige. Her inner ear crackled as the noise-cancellation took effect, too, barring her and Seren from outside sound and vice-versa. The "headspace" mode of modern offices, promoting deeper concentration for higher productivity.

Seren apparently detected the shift in atmosphere as well, immediately flicking her head to the side, then slowly turning to face Emmeline with grave eyes.

"It's all right. Have a seat." Emmeline gestured to a pair of taupe sofas. "Tea? Or perhaps something to ease any, ah, discomfort you might—"

"No. No, thank you. I'm fine." Seren rigidly sat as directed, smoothing the skirt over her thighs. She had shed her lab coat for the day.

Following suit, Emmeline unbuttoned her blazer and laid it on the back of the opposite sofa. She then seated herself in front of it, only belatedly aware of laying a hand on her belly as she did so. She eyed the scientist's skirt and heels. "I hope you only dressed for the meeting."

"Oh." Seren meekly ducked her head as she tucked a loose strand behind her ear. Her hair clip had succumbed to gravity since the morning. "Well, I usually do"—she gestured up and down at her outfit as if to say *dress this way.*

"But in the lab? Be comfortable. Our policy doesn't dictate—"

"I know." She smiled softly. "I *am* comfortable." She looked down at her shoes and, toes together, slid her ankles out and in. "I just like them."

"As long as you know it's your choice."

"I do."

A pause lingered as they just grinned awkwardly at each other.

"Thank you," Seren emphasized again. "I only came here to explain that I'm—"

"Unreaped?" Emmeline fought to keep a calm face as her heart raced.

"What? No! I mean"—she flashed an automatic smile despite a shallow crease between her brows—"yes. Of course I am."

Closing her eyes, Emmeline tipped her chin up. "You know I'll find out another way. This one's better."

Seren held her stare, her plastic grin now twitching at the corner.

Folding her hands, Emmeline leaned forward. "Ms. Singh, *have* you been reaped?"

Blinking, Seren said nothing.

"You aren't used to discussing this openly. I understand. And I'm sorry to be so direct, though you know it's within my rights."

Her mouth still parted on her last word, Seren looked to the floor, a tremor in her lower lip as she said, "There are reasons a woman could still—and you can't assume that just because I—that I… Just look at my record."

"I have done, and it doesn't mention any elective surgery or medication. Nothing…permanent. I know the exceptions, but you must appreciate the rarity. It's ritual without reason."

Which begged the question of the day: Why a professional woman would *choose* to bleed without biological purpose. Call yourself a traditionalist or spiritualist, and you were just as scorned as the unreaped and unemployed.

Looking up, Seren met Emmeline's stare, only shifting her face a minute degree.

"Did you bypass the Harvest altogether," Emmeline asked, "or was it interrupted?"

Seren pursed her lips and dropped her gaze. But Emmeline sensed her defenses lowering, so she waited patiently.

"I'm…" Seren eventually began, "mostly reaped."

"But?"

"I didn't complete my second-year cycles."

Emmeline squinted.

Eyes scanning the floor, Seren swallowed.

"Your record states our Ukraine branch carried out the Harvest. In full," Emmeline said. "Did you meet your husband there, or did you know each other before then?"

Seren blanched. "I met him there."

"He was the nurse assigned to your cycles."

"Yes."

"Did he modify your data?"

The young woman's eyes welled, and she ran a finger beneath her flared nostrils. Moving to her side, Emmeline took one of her hands.

"Seren," she said softly, "I'm asking, not accusing."

The scientist snorted.

"Do you know why I'm not?"

Shrugging, Seren murmured, "Not really if you're going to sack me anyway."

Emmeline huffed a bittersweet laugh through her nose as her lips wavered somewhere between a pout and smile.

Then she pressed her colleague's hand to her stomach.

Seren furrowed her brow at the intimate gesture, but as she looked from their hands to Emmeline's eyes, then back and forth, her watery eyes widened. "No."

Emmeline raised and lowered her chin — slowly, pointedly. "You're the first to know," she said, her eyes filling, too.

"Oh, go on." Seren released her hand and shook her head. "You're having a laugh."

"Can't imagine what's so funny." Her jaw steeled.

Of course, with the right sort of padding, she *could* be bluffing just to ferret out the truth. Wouldn't be the first time employers had tried that, and Emmeline's word would weigh more if it came to one against the other. Yet it would also put her under more scrutiny by the Directors, and she'd had enough of that already.

The scientist dropped her eyes back to the tiled floor and darted them side to side. But Emmeline's gamble wasn't in vain, as with only a moment's further hesitation, Seren exhaled, "Okay. I can hardly understand why, but I believe you, Ms. Frey."

"Please. Emmeline."

"Emmeline."

"But *how?*" Seren hissed, the rest of her words garbled under her breath.

"Well, for starters, I skipped my Harvest as well."

"But *you* of all people…"

"Now you understand my risk." Emmeline leaned back and cupped her hands over her modest bump. "And I yours — in the event I'm right?"

Slowly, Seren bobbed her head.

"So is it your intention to have children as well? Traditionally?"

Seren flinched at the word and seemed to fold into herself again, arms crossed over her lap as her posture deflated. "W-we fell in love so young, so early in our careers. But we both knew we wanted a family. Someday, together." A tear dropped from her eyelashes. "Artem was completely open to bearing—and I didn't oppose that either," she rushed to add, "but…"

"You wanted the option for yourself."

Meeting Emmeline's gaze, Seren's face broke as she nodded.

Emmeline reached for her hand again, this time taking both. "And do you still?"

"Yes," Seren winced, her forearms quivering.

"And Artem's on board."

"Yes."

"Knowing the penalty."

"Yes."

"This could cost his job, too. Have you both looked into wage work, for when the time comes?"

"He has, but I-I don't know. I'd like to keep working, but…"

"You want the option."

Tears streaming now, Seren croaked out, "Yes."

Emmeline wrapped an arm around her shoulders, gave her a side hug, then rubbed the young woman's upper back. "It's still legal. And natural, gaidammit," she added under her breath. That was easy to forget in their sphere, but it was still so. She stopped stroking and gripped Seren's shoulder instead. "We need to keep it so."

Staring intently, she watched Seren breathe herself into a calmer state.

"But…how?"

A great question. One that Emmeline had pondered at length without any clear answers yet, except for the biggest one: she wanted a child. And to bear it herself. Just getting pregnant had surpassed her wildest expectations. Now she had to see it through—within the belly of the beast.

This wasn't a beast to slay, though. Emmeline believed in her family's business, the greater good it achieved. FerLiberté had paved a way to freedom for women that traditional fertility clinics couldn't, daring to consider—and accomplish—childbirth by men.

It was easier than most had realized. Naturally, males weren't equipped with the reproductive organs necessary to conceive and carry a child, but that wasn't to say they didn't have the aptitude nor inclination to. Early signs of their emotional readiness had begun to emerge in the late twentieth and early twenty-first centuries, when "Mr. Moms" increased in number so wives could work full-time. Men, it turned out, were only too relieved to hand over the pressure of being the breadwinner.

This domestic arrangement hadn't suited everyone, but women became overwhelmingly frustrated with the social barriers holding them back. So they fought, and kept fighting, and though it took time, they chipped and chipped away until they could break through to equal employment and income, becoming the new leaders of industry and politics. Maternity benefits improved accordingly.

Even over a century ago in England, Emmeline's grandmother had received good leave. A year off, with six-months' pay and an on-ramp right back to where she'd left off at a leading global bank. Same job, title, salary, and benefits. No detriment to her career.

Until it was. When, after an entire year off work, Emmeline's granny returned to the office to find that her subordinates had advanced into superiors. When, after her second child—Emmeline's mother—she fell further behind even after only taking six months off. The bank had honored its policies, but the lost time caught up to her in performance reviews. It seemed so unfair, criticizing her decreased output after she'd only exercised the generous aid accorded to her. Companies could improve leave time and pay as much as employees demanded, but stop-and-start advancement would always be a problem. And even when benefits packages began to include freezing eggs for later, working women grew tired of having to wait.

That's why, years later, Emmeline's mother Alice realized the issue was no longer social but biological. Until men could bear children, this would always be woman's plight.

And so, science made it happen. Thanks to an embryonic sac implanted into any willing male, harvested eggs fertilized with his or another man's sperm could be brought to full-term inside his own body. Vital nutrients were administered regularly via a port, akin to those used for chemotherapy way back when cancer still hadn't been cured. FerLiberté had pioneered the technology, and Emmeline was its first success.

She had no contact with the male surrogate who'd birthed her from one of her mom's frozen eggs. And her mother — already well beyond childbearing age when Emmeline was born — had since passed. But Alice Frey had seen to the girl's education in England before grooming her at French headquarters. FerLiberté was everything Emmeline knew, her birthright. Yet in her mother's stead, she still had to answer to Madame Inspector and the Directors. And what answers could she offer now.

Emmeline stood and began pacing beside the windows to outside. She flicked her hand up to let in a square of natural light. "I turned forty this year, you know."

"No," Seren said. "I didn't."

"Right." She chuckled toward her chest. Women no longer had to disclose their ages in the workplace, to avoid arbitrary judgment of their value. So Emmeline never had to fudge her record in that regard. In fact, she hadn't overridden any data since that isolated time nineteen years ago, when her mother had brought her on board at the world's first FerLiberté clinic. "I was twenty-one when I started here, just before the Directors mandated the Harvest."

"But your mum. Didn't she still make you do it?"

Emmeline grinned. "Clearly *you* know the ways round that. Not easy, but…"

"Possible."

"I honestly think the hardest bit's smuggling the sodding tampons in. Ah, before I forget…" She walked to her desk and rapidly tapped a code out on its surface. She heard a latch release, then slid out a narrow compartment. Snatching a few tampons and liners, she emptied a condom box and stuffed them into it.

"They know to check these containers at the scans, so this is just for stowing here. Don't attempt anything through building security outside of your person." Lifting the sleeve of prophylactics, she said, "These work for me. Need some?"

"No, I'm good."

As Emmeline figured. Menstrual artifacts might be relegated to the black market after diminished demand all but killed supply, but condoms still sold in abundance. For all the advancements in medicine, venereal disease remained a risk if pregnancy didn't.

"Good. I try to bring in whatever I can, when I can, so whatever you can't manage, you've got backup here. I'll connect you with my supplier, too."

Seren exhaled heavily. "Thank you. I still can't believe this. What you're doing, it's…"

"Insane."

"Inspired."

She wondered if her mother would think so. If all Emmeline was doing, in fact, was *un*doing. Setting women back, after all they'd done, all they'd fought for. All that she and Seren had benefitted from, and those like them — the privileged that society invested in. The educated employed, the ones signing the social contract to work in their fields of study for their entire work-age lives. Productive citizens who yielded return on the knowledge and resources advanced to them.

So while this began with a personal desire — to be a natural mother — Emmeline realized the impact of her position. This was greater than her. She realized it from the moment she'd tired of improvising her own sanitary items and sought supplies on the fringe. Concealing who she was, she'd met the women of the underworld, and the men who supported or exploited them. They peddled both counterfeits and the real deal, sourced from scant inventories. Some even made their fair share off cruder homemade solutions.

Many she encountered were among the disadvantaged, who'd never had access to reaping even if they'd wanted it. But there was also the Uterine Underground, those who'd *opted out*, sacrificing career progression, social status, and a financial penalty for "wasting" their formal education and workplace training. Even though central authorities hadn't passed the Harvest as law themselves, they endorsed their private and public enterprises to promote healthy economies. And by now, to reduce recruiting, training, opportunity, and maternity costs, most institutions did require that fertile female candidates have all eggs harvested by their start date—even better, by the time they applied. In large credit to FerLiberté's innovation, the Harvest could be completed in under two years.

The conditions she saw among the outcast mothers had almost scared Emmeline from her shameful fancies. At one point, she'd been about to hop a plane to Spain and start a secret Harvest there. But there was one force she couldn't fight: maternal instinct.

"I started inseminating myself a year ago," she said, since she didn't have a partner. "After hours. I figured it wouldn't take straight away, and it didn't. But then—Fourteenth of July, fittingly enough. France's Independence Day became mine, too. But Bastille Day's really about *unity*, isn't it, not separation. I'm not trying to strike out on my own."

Emmeline paused in her pacing and leaned against the sunlit window.

"I just want women to have a choice."

Standing at the front desk in FerLiberté's lobby, Madame Inspector smiled up at the imposing but glorious statue. Her gaze caressed the graceful copper folds of the flowing gown, up to the great book in the lady's left hand and then the gleaming torch in her right.

Head craned back on her neck, Madame proceeded to pan her sight along the atrium's upper levels. The corners of her lips twitched down when she saw the opaque windows to Frey's headspace.

Her duty there long since completed, Madame Inspector could've left hours ago. But as they'd conducted the routine inspection so far ahead of year-end this time, she'd bade her team to run another quick once-over for good measure. She didn't want the Directors to think she'd rushed the job.

And there beyond a wall of beige was her precise reason for carrying things out so early. The inspection might be annual, but Madame Inspector's responsibilities were daily—overseeing all clinics globally, but she had particular interest in this one.

Brought under Alice Frey's wing many years ago, her loyalty, unlike her mentor, was undying. On Alice's passing, she was entrusted to step in where the elder Frey had stepped out—but without stepping on the younger Frey's toes. Yet Madame found Alice somewhat lax in her expectations for the girl, or at least too trusting that Emmeline would carry on the mission with as much fervor. The offspring had inherited her mother's scientific and business acumen, but did Madame detect an air of sentimental whim as well? A love of literature and recreation that never seemed to occupy Alice as much? Were the girl's holidays, perhaps, also longer than necessary? Her desire to escape to the countryside or work from home becoming more common? Her work hadn't suffered from it, of course, but still.

Frey was losing her focus. Her temperament was distractible, her dietary intake becoming indulgent. And now she and her lab scientist were meeting once more in clandestine fashion. She suspected it but didn't know it until she removed her tablet from her case, tapped into the security feed and replayed the moment the young woman had disappeared into Frey's headspace. A pity cameras in non-communal spaces were illegal.

She'd so like to watch the feed from that restroom, too. Especially now, after her team had gone back and swabbed the elevator's glass floor.

By the time Seren left and Emmeline cleared her headspace walls, the "Suffergettes" still had no defined game plan. They'd come up with that nickname, at least, when laughing over their *choice* to suffer menstrual and natal pain. Gaia, did it feel so free to share empathy. Emmeline also offered Seren more advice on cheating the daily body scans and quarterly urine tests.

How to pass the scans going forward, though, was more problematic for Emmeline. Hiding her growth had been easy so far. She hadn't shown through her first trimester and only barely had a bump now. Going into the winter, she could conceal herself beneath bulkier clothes and behind bags and tables as much as possible—"like pregnant actors did on those retro television-device shows," she'd told Seren. The scanner might also only reveal weight gain for a time, but they considered the possibility of hacking into it, eventually, to manipulate imaging. Something to research over the coming weeks, tapping the talents of the Uterine Underground.

In the meantime, Emmeline followed a self-imposed protocol and worked harder and longer than ever—openly blaming that for stress-eating and weight gain. She volunteered this information whenever the time seemed right, since no one could ask what she knew they were thinking. At least her naturally curvy stature seemed to work to her advantage, camouflaging the physical changes better than petite Seren might be able to. Hopefully when that day came, Seren wouldn't have to hide and could instead flaunt her maternity with pride in the FerLiberté lab.

With her colleague's covert help at present, though, Emmeline felt infinitely more optimistic. She hadn't thought everything through when she'd first conceived the idea, let alone the child. But her plan came into sharper view in the New Year, and the more she learned from the Underground, the more a plan B took shape, too.

Whatever would come, she was determined to make it to March.

I give her until March, Madame Inspector thought. She didn't know when the Frey baby was due, exactly, but before long, the expecting mother should be too big to hide it.

Thank goodness, in the meantime, that based on all the observations Madame had detailed for them—including how loose dresses had replaced Frey's smart suits—the Directors granted her clearance for investigation. A private one.

By design, one's headspace couldn't be tampered with, but urine traps, for example, were easy enough to install in communal employee toilets. Anything collected and tested couldn't be used as legal evidence, even if it did prove Frey's breach of contract, but the Directors would take no internal disciplinary action against Madame's methods. These gentlewomen knew as well as she that, given enough time, Frey would give her*self* up.

She'll be forced to show herself for the traitor she is. And I'll be there when she does.

"Vive la liberté! Vive FerLiberté!"

Splaying a hand toward the wall screen, Emmeline pinched her fingers together to zap out the newscast.

Yet *"Vive la liberté! Vive FerLiberté!"* persisted outside, rising from the atrium floor to hum against her headspace windows.

Mother's Day.

At least in the UK it was. France's *Fête des Mères* would come a couple of months later, but with the sizable expat community in Paris—and considering FerLiberté's own British origins—both days were informally celebrated as Woman's Independence Day. Why have only one anyway, when *every* day was hers to seize.

As was tradition the Friday before each such holiday, employees and members of the public assembled in FerLiberté's lobby to exalt *la statue de la Liberté.* Women and their supporters raised proud fists to her in *liberté, égalité, et fraternité.* Emmeline couldn't think of a better time to share her news than in this spirit of sisterhood.

The news crews were positioned below in anticipation of her bi-annual speech. Above the statue and stopped at Emmeline's floor, the glass elevator awaited her. Its curved wall panes were already collapsed—like a telescope—to below the railing, opening the lift to the air like a balcony. She would ride it down to just above the statue and, from this vantage, expose what she could no longer veil through strategic clothing, positioning, hiding, hacking, holidaying, or working from home. Emmeline was eight months along. She felt it, and she looked it.

"I'll stand next to the fountain," Seren told her, "if you need to look at me for courage. I'll be there for you, smiling you through it." Just as she had been.

The two Suffergettes stood in Emmeline's headspace, putting the finishing touches on her makeup.

"Be happy," Seren said when Emmeline's breathing became labored. "What you're doing is wonderful. Natural. For yourself, for us."

Biting her lip, Emmeline nodded, then ran a fingertip across where she'd mussed her lipstick.

She channeled her nervous energy into rubbing her round stomach. Beneath the dress's green silk, occasional kicks consoled her. She wasn't in this alone. She hadn't been and she wouldn't be.

The long-sleeved maxi dress looked quite fetching, too. It covered her conservatively yet outlined her contours well enough to show she had nothing to hide.

"I'll head down," Seren said.

She exited the headspace as Emmeline turned back to the wall she'd mirrored. She draped a large wool wrap around her shoulders and over her waist. Made her final adjustments. Practiced her speech to her reflection. After stalling another few minutes, she flicked her hand upward, and the mirrored surface turned transparent.

Emmeline breathed in deeply, then tapped the door open to set foot into the hall.

"Mademoiselle Frey, I will need you to come with me, please."

Madame Inspector couldn't help the smirk that accompanied her derogatory use of *mademoiselle*. The look on Frey's face made her grin even wider.

"My apologies," Madame said as two tall women grasped each of Frey's biceps from behind, "but you won't be giving this year's Mother's Day speech. Nor the *Fête des Mères* or any after, I'm afraid."

"What are you doing?" Frey snarled as she struggled. "Let go of me!"

The ends of her wrap slipped to her sides, letting her stomach protrude between them. Madame flattened her palm against it, felt the firm membrane and movement, and nodded her cue to stick the syringe in Frey's neck.

"We will...when we have you where we want you."

"No!" Frey kicked as they escorted her down the hall, toward the service elevator that would permit a furtive exit to the black hover cars waiting at the clinic's back street. The injected dose would sedate her, but only gradually; she should enter a twilight by the time they reached their transport downstairs. They didn't want her losing consciousness now on her feet, obligating them to drag her heavy load, as carrying her prostrate would be too conspicuous, were anyone to see.

Madame could only hope all camera crews had obeyed the directive to remain at lobby level or mezzanine. She hadn't wanted to cut it this close, but as Frey had remained out of the office on sick leave recently—and communicated electronically that her second-in-command was ready to preside over today's event, if necessary—Madame couldn't be certain of her intentions. By the time anyone had arrived that morning, Frey had already sealed herself within her opaque headspace. And as witnessed only moments ago when they'd passed in the hall, the scientist had been in there as well, that filthy, low-class bleeder. This would be the end of her career, too. But Singh wasn't their biggest concern just now.

And so, Madame Inspector had laid the trap and awaited her rat.

"No," Emmeline repeated with weakening body but not resolve.

They'd drugged her, actually drugged her *and* her baby. She needed Seren, needed a way.

Approaching the end of the hall and turning the corner, she surmised they'd go for the service elevator just past the atrium one. After her initial fight response, she'd slackened her arms with hope her guards would loosen their grip in turn. They only needed to by just enough…

Enough.

Summoning all her strength and more — that superhuman power of a mother's love, she knew on instinct — Emmeline ripped herself from her captors, slipping out from the wool wrap in their hands and propelling herself into the glass elevator. She caught herself at the railing, actually bending over it from the momentum, but quickly commanded the doors to shut. They closed on a few furious arms, but the doors were to the floor itself, not a part of the elevator, which now lowered on her demand. The arms above snatched out as fast as possible before the glass ceiling could break them.

Arriving level with the statue's glistening flame, Emmeline felt the fire inside her. She stopped the lift between floors, then stepped to the railing with one hand on her belly and the other upheld in a fist. The crowd below her exploded in applause and cheers.

"*Vive la liberté! Vive FerLiberté!*" started up again. The jumbo screens along the walls flickered like indoor fireworks.

Heaving as she caught her breath, Emmeline released a laugh, her face wet with sweat and tears. She kissed her hand and extended it out to them, then aimed another air-kiss at Seren, who stood next to the fountain, right where she'd promised to be. The two held each other's gaze, laughing and crying together.

Their unspoken understanding was so full of hope and light in that moment, of all that could be, that Emmeline didn't even notice the chants and claps taper off until she saw Seren knit her brow and break eye contact to look around. The smile vanished from her face.

The cheers went silent in a rolling wave.

"*Nom de* Gaia," echoed from somewhere. "*Mon Dieu*," from somewhere else.

"Hypocrite!" was lobbed out next. "*C'est une traîtresse!*"

More cries of "Traitor!" and "Disgrace!" erupted around the room. Others like "This is an outrage!" and "How dare you!" soon followed, peppered with increasing screams of "*Salope*" and "*Connasse*," which Emmeline didn't need French fluency to understand.

The crowd roiled with boos and shouts.

"No!" she pleaded against her growing fatigue. "You don't understand!"

Mingled in the cacophony were cries for her resignation.

"That's not necessary," she said, attempting to smile and recall bits of her speech. "I've balanced my duties perfectly fine so far and *shall* continue to. I still believe in FerLiberté with everything I am!"

"*Ferme ta gueule!*"

"Sod off!"

"But I can do both!" she cried. "*We* can! Why shouldn't we have it all?"

"We already do!" someone called out. "Without stooping to *this!*" The woman's face contorted with disgust.

"Go find a man to support you!" someone else jeered.

"B-But…if a woman wants a career and family," Emmeline said, faltering yet determined, "and *wants* to do it herself, she should have the right, shouldn't she? And she should have the right to *not* want both. Just family, I mean. And bear her children and raise them at home if she chooses." Looking around,

Emmeline panted. "These women have been marginalized, and for what? Believing our bodies should still do something a man's can't on its own doesn't mean our brains can't still do what a man's does. We have *both*, the best of *both* worlds. Why take that away from ourselves? Why—" A numbing wave washed over her, and she lost her footing for a moment. Leaning forward and clutching the railing, she swallowed, then continued, "Why writhe for what we wished for?"

"*We* aren't," someone yelled.

"We—" Emmeline lost her air. Hunching, she gripped the rail and sharply inhaled. "Women fought so hard for *liberté* and *égalité*," she whimpered, then shouted with everything she had, "Where is the *fraternité?*" Her full weight against the railing, her head and chest heaved with her struggling breath. She couldn't feel her legs, but while everything else slowed down, the life kicked inside of her. "Wh—when did… Since when does our right to choose"—she started to slip down the lift's lower partition, her voice falling out of earshot—"mean not getting to choose?" Reaching bottom, she slumped against the polycarbonate, her cheek smashed to the clear surface as she mumbled, "Since when do women not support other women?"

Through the smudge left by her sinking face, she could see Seren's slight figure edge its way out of the crowd and toward the lobby doors. Away from Emmeline. The blurred faces in her wake congealed into one massive, angry, roaring throat, ready to consume.

She curled into fetal. Her heart ceased hammering in her chest, slowing with her breath. All noise cancelled out, except for a ringing in her ears.

Losing focus, she saw Alice's eyes emerge from the haze. Clear blue, sharp with ambition but sparked with passion…not the ashen-grey glare overseeing her legacy now.

No, in her mother's eyes, Emmeline saw the skies above a last hope for freedom.

Plan B.

A motion in the corner of her eye alerted her to Madame Inspector's team of women, climbing in through the gaps from both floors now that they'd managed to force open the doors. Seizing Emmeline yet again, they yanked her to her feet. She couldn't hear their barks. With lolling head, she just stared as they commanded the elevator to ground level.

On the way down, a tide surged against their feet, drowning all view below as her water broke against the glass floor.

Château de Vascœuil, France

In the rural quiet of a crisp March night, the Society gathered.

A low din filled the dining room. A fire crackled, and silver knives scraped and clanked against china, slicing through bloody meat and the deep murmur of discussion. Grey heads and black ties ringed the long banquet table. At the head of it sat a white-bearded man.

Wiping his mouth with a cloth napkin, he slid his heavy chair back to stand. He clinked his crystal goblet with a dessert spoon.

"Gentlemen," he said, then cleared his throat. "Needless to say, it appears matters haven't gone *quite* as planned. We anticipated rebellion, of course, but dare I say, no one saw this one coming."

This met with animated mutterings around the table, sharing surprise and disdain. There was much they needed to discuss tonight, regarding one Emmeline Frey. They'd need to ensure the Directors dealt with her exit from the corporation properly and that the media spun this right.

They would also have to investigate and dismantle this countryside commune they'd learned of—the one that, according to a source, Mademoiselle Frey kept referring to as "Plan B" in her delirium at the hospital. A collective of enterprising unreaped women, apparently, who'd united in exile at a village just a few hours outside Paris. Frey had funneled money to them over recent months, as deeper investigation into her accounts confirmed. Education and training *not* entirely gone to waste, the settlement evidently thrived well enough that Frey'd planned to live there herself if she ever left FerLiberté by choice or force. Who knew how many others like it existed, but those they could deal with. Emmeline Frey, on the other hand…

"She is but one woman," the speaker continued, "but she is *that* woman. The very posterchild for woman's liberation. The most significant stride our council has made in preserving and enhancing man's dominance in society."

For the most part, they'd succeeded. Comprised of politicians, executives, professors, lawyers, scientists, philosophers, high-ranking military, and the like, the Society had done exemplary work in recent generations — advising and encouraging females to fulfill their potential and rise to leadership roles. It was in the last century this had markedly taken effect, when the wise council of men undertook to relieve the world's Eves of their reproductive responsibilities.

"Women wouldn't see it this way, certainly, and of course isn't that the point, gentlemen?"

More mutters of agreement and guffaws followed, punctuated by one "Hear, hear!"

All that women did perceive — as the Society saw it — were progressive men supporting their cause. Or supportive women who'd been encouraged by progressive men supporting their cause. Or women who'd been encouraged by *those* women. And so on and so forth.

But not all "progressive" men were in earnest, and that's where the secret Society factored in. Their influence expanded exponentially, from their elite number to their female friends, colleagues, cousins, wives, daughters, sisters, aunts, and nieces — and then from those women to *their* female friends, colleagues, cousins, wives, daughters, sisters, aunts, and nieces. And so on. The network reached and tied together the fields of science, business, politics, media, academia, and law—the diverse areas in which the Society excelled and could pull their puppets' strings.

The Directors at FerLiberté were an ideal case in point. They believed they ran things, but who were they, really, but the Society's female friends, colleagues, cousins, wives, daughters, sisters, aunts, nieces, or extensions of such—indeed, mere extensions of the Society!

"And so, we've allowed—nay, *encouraged*—woman to ascend within each 'lever' of power, ambition blinding her to whose hand is still on that lever."

"Would you say it still is, though, sir?" a man among them ventured. "I tend to see a very real shift in power as female career progression coincides with male regression. No one could've anticipated the percentage of males so keen on giving birth, though we'd certainly hoped. But now this seems to be at the expense of what women historically faced: men increasingly in low-status, low-paying jobs, or leaving top roles for paternity leave, part-time, or stay-at-home-parenting. Might we have inadvertently impaired man's ambition and opportunity to advance?"

"Mm," the speaker grunted as he stroked his beard. "You raise an astute point, and I'm not oblivious to this trend. Nor, in fact, did I not anticipate it. Need I remind you of our mission. Throughout history, man has been able to dominate every position of power—except the one that nature denied us. So, what I see occurring now is simply the exercise of man's choice, now that he finally has the freedom to choose."

The best of both worlds—and to be the best at them. *That* was what they sought.

Which was why, as each vintage luxury car with wheels had rolled into the drive that evening, *La Victoire de la Liberté* was the first to welcome them to Vascoeuil Castle. A remnant of the property's days as an art and history center, Salvador Dali's twentieth-century sculpture was almost an exact replica of Bartholdi's Statue of Liberty.

Almost.

This Lady Liberty held not one but *two* torches, with both arms raised. Cheering. Triumphant. Seizing enlightenment and life with both hands.

The Society speaker raised his glass to toast their fine victory.

"Now, gentlemen, we really do have it all."

"The Glass Floor" was written in 2017 for Brick Moon Fiction's themed call for submission: "Liberty." Among other criteria, the Statue of Liberty was essential, so I chose the replica that stands on Paris's Île aux Cygnes in real life. The Salvador Dali version—holding two torches—also exists at the actual Vascoeuil Castle in France. I got the idea for FerLiberté from the challenges and shaming faced by working and stay-at-home parents alike, and it's fair to say I took great "liberty" indeed with this fantastical scenario.

Used with permission of Brick Moon Fiction.

Part III

Mystic

Reality TV

A vignette.

"**I**s this the room where you were murdered?"
Thud.

Screams.

Beeeeep! "What the—" *Beeeep!*

A blue-grey face with white hair stood motionless with its mouth gaping open and reflective eyes widened. It exchanged unintelligible whispers with another illuminated figure until a caption read, *Bloody hell, did you hear that?*

"Knock again if you were bludgeoned he—"

Tap.

Gasps.

"Oh, what the—" *beep!* "—was that?"

Beeeep!

More screams.

"Precisely what you asked for," the aged innkeeper muttered to her television set. "You've been doing this for years, you say? And you're still that scared? Not buyin' it."

Violins screeched to a menacing crescendo as teasers for the ghost-hunting show's next scenes flashed on the screen. "In part two of *Highly Haunted*," a British male voice announced, "Lynette Spaulding leads her team into the pub cellar, where staff have reported the most paranormal activity." His words were punctuated by a Morse Code of more beeps and shrieks from Lynette and her crew before the show then cut to commercial.

With a sigh, Anna Bosworth raised her remote and surfed the channels away from the UK reality show. She could barely tolerate Lynette's profession, let alone her theatrical fright. Surely no one *that* afraid of ghosts would still be in the business of pursuing them.

As it stood, guests had reported a lot of paranormal activity at Anna's inn as well. But such was the charm of an old house's history, and she didn't mind the rumors if they encouraged people to visit the Otto Byrd Country Haus, not scare them off.

But scaring people off was precisely what the Wee Wanderer shop in town had feared when it recently turned away a ghost-hunting TV program interested in investigating customer claims. Now, Anna didn't believe in ghosts and would've never imagined soliciting a supernatural service herself. But she did tend to think any publicity for a small business was good publicity, so she found the Wee Wanderer's decision to turn away the Hotel In-Spectres very foolish indeed.

Especially when they rarely investigated anywhere but hospitality lodgings like hotels and inns; for them to be interested in the Wee Wanderer store, the alleged paranormal activity must've been impressive—or at least would've made for good ratings. Or maybe it was enough that the vintage shop had once been a residence where people did sleep…and die. The Otto Byrd Country Haus could claim the same. And now the Hotel In-Spectres had Anna curious.

Anna had never watched any shows like this before so didn't know what, exactly, she'd be undertaking were she to actually contact the Hotel In-Spectres herself. Likely she wouldn't, but for fun, at least—and with all of her guests turned in for tonight—she'd retired here to her private quarters to see what the fuss was about.

According to the TV guide, another station was airing *Hotel In-Spectres* in a few minutes, so Anna stopped at its channel, then left to prepare some chamomile tea in the meantime.

By the time she sat back down, leaving her tea to cool in its delicate china cup on the table beside her, two team members onscreen were sitting in what appeared to be a bedroom. At first glance, their routine looked similar to *Highly Haunted*'s, but so far, this team was far less skittish. And better at watching their language.

The scene cut to another room with a different pair of investigators.

"Okay, so we're here in the dining hall of Highgate House," one investigator informed viewers. He glowed like a negative photo from the camera's night-vision setting, and a caption in the lower right corner identified him as Gavin, with *@GavGotGhost* beneath his name. Even Anna knew that was an online handle, now that modern times and a low marketing budget had forced the Byrd Haus into the social-media sphere.

"This is where we're told visitors and employees often see a shadowy figure and hear a man's voice," Gavin said. "We want to find out if this spirit is a threat to the occupants or just wants them to know it's here. Or instead of something that can intelligently interact with us, it could simply be residual energy playing itself over and over like a recording. And, as always, we'll be looking to see if the phenomena could be debunked by a natural explanation."

Pursing her lips, Anna nodded at this conservative approach. *Natural* explanations she could accept, and she would bet that was usually the case for the Hotel In-Spectres—that or fake evidence. She blew on her tea, sipped it, then snuggled into her green velvet armchair as the two team members settled themselves at a dinner table and placed a small flashlight at its center.

"The flashlight is highly sensitive to touch," the female investigator explained as *Tracy* and *@TrackerTracy* faded in and out of the corner of the TV screen. "So, it should be very simple for the spirit to turn it on and off." As a test, she lightly tapped the device a couple of times herself, which turned it on and off accordingly. "But we'll start with the basics."

After a little more chitchat between themselves, and adjustments to their camcorder and another piece of handheld equipment that Anna couldn't identify, the soul-searching duo commenced their line of questioning.

"Is there anyone in here with us?" Tracy asked.

She waited for a response.

"Is there anyone here? Knock twice if you can hear us."

A long pause, then…

Knock-knock.

Neither investigator reacted to the sound. They just continued looking around as though still waiting for the answer they'd already been given.

"Are you here with us? Knock twice if you are."

Knock-knock.

The investigators still didn't respond, but a few seconds later, there was a high-pitched creak, which they both immediately turned their heads toward.

"What was that?" Tracy whispered. "Did you hear it, too? Like a creaking sound?"

Gavin nodded. "Yeah, it sounded like it was over by the window."

Anna pinched her brows at how they could hear that yet still hadn't said anything about the knocks. Even she'd heard them clear as day.

"Hold on." Tracy got up to approach the window. There was another creak as soon as she peered outside of it. "Oh." Walking back to the table, she said, "It's a flagpole mounted on the exterior wall. It squeaks when the wind blows."

"Debunked!" Gavin raised his hand for a high-five when Tracy sat back down. "Okay, so that wasn't you," he said, presumably to the spirit, "but can you knock twice if you're here?"

Knock-knock.

Anna whipped her head to her right, where she thought she'd heard the sound this time. "Yes?" she asked, in case it was a guest needing something.

No one answered.

"Can you knock just once?" Gavin asked from the TV.

Knock.

Anna heard it come from her door again. So she got up to open it, but no one was there. The old mansion's acoustics could be weird, though, so maybe it was someone moving around in a room upstairs, or maybe it had come from the TV show after all. Anna could swear, though, that the sounds had come from the hallway's direction. Just in case, she left the door ajar for anyone who might need her, before returning to her seat in front of the television.

"Let's use the flashlight," Tracy whispered to Gavin, then explained to viewers that the flashlight technique was usually the most effective with shy spirits. "Communicating-with-the-living for beginners, if you will."

"Would that be easier for you?" Gavin asked the open air. "Can you turn the light on for us?"

A table lamp next to Anna flickered, so she made a fleeting mental note to replace the bulb soon. The investigators' light, however, remained off. Anna harrumphed to herself, not surprised, and reached for her tea. And now that she thought about it, the knocking earlier had probably come from other team members inside Highgate House. So maybe Tracy and Gavin *had* heard it and automatically debunked its natural cause. Probably an occupational hazard they'd become used to.

"It's easy. See?" Tracy tapped the flashlight again to turn it on. "Now you try. Can you turn it back off?"

Tracy's flashlight stayed on, but Anna's table lamp went out. Anna looked to her side and tried to recall if she had extra bulbs in the closet. She was about to set her tea down and get up to look when Gavin asked, "Can you flash the light twice if you can hear us?"

The flashlight did nothing, but, within its scalloped ivory shade, Anna's table lamp flickered on, then off, then back on — before all the lights in her sitting room went out.

She gasped but sat still with her teacup and saucer in her hands. The electricity was wonky in this old place. More often than not it was because mice and squirrels chewed on the wires. So, she hoped this was just a blip that would pass momentarily — and that it was limited to her room. She didn't need more guests complaining in online reviews.

Tracy, too, waited patiently before tapping her flashlight again, flashing it on and off a few times. "Do you see what I'm doing? Can you try it, too? Can you turn the light on if you're here and you can hear us?"

The flashlight didn't turn on, but Anna spilled some of her tea in her lap when her room lights all re-illuminated — and then, just as quickly, zapped out to darkness.

With the vintage china clattering in her hands, as the warm liquid seeped through her pale linen trousers, Anna whispered to the lights, "Please turn back on." And they did.

At the same time, the show switched over to two other Hotel In-Spectres investigating the Highgate House library. "Some of the phenomena people reportedly experience here," one man said (Trent, a.k.a. *@ghostgeek2*), "are books falling from the shelves and the sound of children giggling or pages turning."

"Can you let us know you're here?" asked Jacob (*@marleynmarley*). "Can you pull out a book?"

Whump.

As Trent and Jacob looked around with no reaction, Anna stared wide-eyed at the leather-bound novel that had just flown off her own shelf.

"Is there a book that's your favorite?" Trent asked. "Can you show it to us?"

An Agatha Christie paperback landed at Anna's feet, seconds before her teacup and saucer tumbled there as well from her limp, shaking hands.

"As of now, we can't confirm anything in this house to be paranormal," Trent concluded from the TV, while Anna the innkeeper fled from her room.

"Reality TV" isn't a standalone story but, in fact, the draft prologue to The Byrd Haus, *Book One in my prospective* Hotel In-Spectres *series. I've included it here as a sneak peek at the haunted happenings to come with my fictional TV ghost hunters. The next story, "Revolve Her," takes place in the same universe, serving as a prequel of sorts to another book —* The Roche Motel *— that will feature in the series.*

Revolve Her

A novella.

A-Side

July 2018

She watches blood soak into the tatty motel carpet, wondering what it's like to be dead.

"She said...sh-she said..."

Ellie kneels beside his body.

She didn't mean to do this. Can't remember who told her to. Or if this is what she'd—he'd, *they'd*—even said. Just that she, Eleanor, had been the one to do it, and she'd watched it all play out before her like it was onstage.

The doing of it was a bit of a blur, but the after part...the after of it sharpened into high resolution—the life draining from his eyes while the blood spilled from his chest.

And *she* did that, what just happened to this thing, this thing that used to be a person she knew but now lies here inanimate and foreign to her. She still grips the revolver in her damp palm, feels the weight of it angling her hand limply to the side. Her gaze follows where the shiny barrel points to his pocket.

Bugger.

The keys. They bulge beneath his denim, one baring its snout just above the pocket's hem.

She fists her free hand to steady it from its incessant shaking. Then, unclenching it, she eases her long fingers into the still-warm folds of his distressed designer jeans. The pad of her middle finger squeezes past the keyring, which she hooks to draw it out.

There. This foreign thing on the ground won't be needing these anymore. Never did.

Eagerly, she stuffs the keys into her cleavage before wiping her palm along her bare thigh. She stands and drops the gun, notes its absent thud on the puke-colored carpet. How anticlimactic. Its silent descent, just like his, when he'd fallen first to his knees and then on his face, before she turned him over with a grunt so she could watch his blue eyes go blank.

And then it finally hits her. The enormity of it.

No, Ellie doesn't know what it'd be like to be dead. But she does know how it feels to be sad, and right now she doesn't understand why she doesn't. Feel sad. Doesn't *feel*…anything.

Looking around at the beige stucco walls, she knows they couldn't have completely absorbed the sound, that it's only a matter of time before accountability will show up at the motel room door in some form and swallow her whole. Her life will end at thirty, when it has barely begun.

Staring up at the ceiling, she parts her numb lips and says —

"You did this. Why? Why did you make me do this?"

No.

No, no, no. She's wrong.

You can't see me. You can't hear me...can you, Eleanor?

But I didn't do anything. Didn't say anything.

Did I?

Well.

Yes.

Okay.

Maybe I did say something. Willed *it to happen, anyway. But she doesn't understand what I said. And I didn't even know that she could hear me.*

That she would listen.

Yet she hasn't actually done anything, has she? She's just imagining this. Only picturing what it would be like if she did do it—*if she'd have the nerve, really see it through, and if she could stomach it, get away with it, all the details she'd have to sort to secure her freedom. I can see it as her mind sees it. And what she sees is...*

No. I did not tell her to do that. Wouldn't want to bend her will that way—because she doesn't know what it's like to kill or be killed, but she does know what it's like to fight like hell for herself. I suppose I did get carried away in the wave of that, in the flow of my own thoughts. So easy to forget how powerful they are, how powerful they make me. I forget how...

How the thoughts are all I am anymore. Like I've never been born.

Ellie zones out at the ceiling as if she's actually expecting a reply. She knows the voice isn't there, that her accusation falls on her panic-deafened ears only.

"Fuck's sake." She exhales as she looks to the empty floor.

I didn't really do it.

She holds up her hand. Empty as well, has been since she last set her hairbrush down on the bathroom counter. Pressing her palm to her breasts, she feels the keys aren't there either.

The revolver. It must still rest in the confines of her new concealed-carry purse—the green faux-crocodile bag Ellie would never otherwise buy and didn't even bother to haggle over at the swap meet outside of Phoenix. She'd just wanted to get it and get out of there before someone saw her, as if anyone would.

Well, of course someone would; that's all they ever seem to do when you look like Ellie. Her tiny, top-heavy frame can sometimes command the sort of attention she doesn't want, her brassy dyed hair, dark skin, and too-good-to-be-true tits only adding to the stares, the smirks. The slurs. Passing in one respect hasn't given her the key to all clubs. And if there were ever a time she didn't want to be noticed, for better or for worse, it was at a sodding swap meet buying a sodding concealed-carry bag in the middle of the sodding desert. Getting the bloody gun had been easier than that.

Stepping to the door, Ellie cracks it open and flinches at the column of white light stabbing through the narrow gap. Squeezing her eyes closed and feeling a vein pulse in her temple, she sees the glowing starburst dim behind her eyelids and, now adjusted to the Arizona sunlight, swings the door open fully. She leans against its rough wood grain and slumps her shoulders on an exhale.

A sigh of relief. Real relief. Not the twisted release that her deranged vengeance fantasy gave her in that quick, sickening moment of flipping Robert's dead body over like a sack of sand. Sickening only in how *not* sick she felt, standing over him, gun in hand, looking at him-yet-not-him. It was that void that frightened her the most, the absence of remorse or grief after exacting a punishment that didn't fit a crime never committed.

Yes, he'd lied—and by spectacular omission, at that—but she'll get over it. In time. Until then, she just wants her bloody keys back.

Lowering her lids again, Ellie inhales a deep, gritty breath of dry desert air and then reopens her eyes to the distant red rocks. The sky above the buttes is impossibly blue, not a single wisp of cloud attempting to smudge it out.

Good day, Sunshine, she thinks, not one to take this elusive friend for granted, marveling at how the locals must do it every day. This is the quintessential summer morning, here in the States. Not like in the UK, where summer is basically a second spring.

She glances to the side and spies her dusty sedan just outside, exactly where Robert parked it after neon-red *vacancy* had beckoned them to pull into the lot last night. They'd left his house only minutes before then, not slinking off in search of some sultry, sordid rendezvous but in a blaze of glory after a magnificent fight. He'd have surely let the door hit her on her way out after what she'd said, yet refused to let her drive in her condition. After checking her in — as if she couldn't have managed that on her own as well — he escorted her to Room 7 and Ubered back to his own private desert oasis, taking her rental-car keys with him. Just in time to receive his wife into loving arms, no doubt.

That's the convenient detail he'd left out when they first met back in London. He had jet-setted his way in from America for a medical conference full of very important doctor-types like him, letting off steam in a Soho club after the first day of seminars. That's where he bumped into Ellie on her way off the dance floor. And he continued to bump — and grind — into her afterward in one of the darker corner booths, high as they both were on something he'd slipped onto her tongue not long after her name had rolled off it. She'd welcomed it, then slipped her tongue onto his not long after that. And then much later, back at Ellie's flat...

They talked.

Just talked. All night.

Ended the evening the way they wished they'd started it once mutually coming to know this wouldn't be a one-time thing. Robert was in town the entire week and devoted every day of it to her. Just her. He skipped all but his own seminars and forewent his five-star hotel for her third-floor flat.

Tucked away in their own little corner of St. John's Wood, they'd cook curry and dal as they sipped on wine and drank from each other's affections. They'd go from gentle to fierce and back to gentle lovemaking in Ellie's bed, bath, and beyond, entangled in the eclectic patterns draped all over her small flat. Making love all day long, her heart singing songs it never knew the words to before. And how Ellie would literally hum when he kissed from her knee to her upper thigh, tracing tattoos with his tongue until he reached and praised the medical mastery that invited him in so willingly. Together, they'd undulate in synchronous rhythm, coming down from the cloud to nestle in a haze of cigarette smoke instead, cuddling and whispering. They took such pleasure, too, in just giggling together by the window at tourists, whose steady pilgrimage to a famous zebra crossing caused such nuisance for street traffic.

And such was how Ellie fell a bit in love with Dr. Robert Rigby by the end of one week. How a tosser who'd used his swagger to drug her in a club had come to mean anything more than a rebound snog and shag.

And why she'd invited him to her North London parlor—Ink & Intuition—to tattoo his virgin, suntanned skin with her name so he'd never forget. He never did get inked, though, claiming fear of her needle. A surgeon, afraid of needles.

Now, she can only hope her top artist will conjure something clever back at the shop, a classy yet quick fix to mask the name of an arse that presently graces her actual arse. So many punters who pop into Ellie's shop for consultations love the idea of tattoos but fear the permanence of them. What if they change their minds? What if they outgrow it and regret it? She'd never pressure someone into getting one if they weren't ready, though she also never thought she'd relate so well to their fears. And since when was she so sentimental, so cliché in her own profession? Never again would a man claim such prime real estate on her body.

Robert, for one, had more than enough territory of his own to piss on. She didn't expect his house to go on seemingly for miles with all the rooms, garage spaces, fountains, and statuary to be found in and around that terracotta palace. When Ellie first arrived in Sedona, she second-guessed whether he'd given her the address to a resort. She even glanced around for signs pointing to a reception office. Never had she seen such a goliath housing one individual. The chapel built into the red rocks above only further took her breath away.

These structures, in combination with the supersaturated color of earth and sky, assaulted her senses yet left her tingling—a heady buzz to be here living the decadent American dream with Robert on a whole new frontier. It was exhilarating. She drank in and gargled every arid drop of this landscape, unable to wait any longer for the terrain she'd next explore indoors, in what had to be Robert's heaven of a bed.

She navigated to what she thought was the front door. *A* door, anyway. Pressing a button on a metal panel, Ellie waited to hear his voice through the speaker.

And heard a woman's instead.

Raising her chin, Ellie now arches away from her motel room's door, sticking out her grade-A breasts as she inhales and laments the fool she's been. She's baring a lot of intricately inked skin in this strategically chosen tank top, her gauzy ikat skirt draping gracefully at her feet. Delicate gold rings encircle a few of her bare toes, and she mocks the vanity of it all. That she allowed herself to wake and dress this morning half-expecting—who is she kidding? *Wholly* expecting—him to knock on her door with urgent remorse. At which point, she would resist and tell him to get fucked, only to carry that command out on him herself after the heat of another argument left her parched and drinking from his special cup again.

And that's when the fantasy took its darker turn.

When the voice rang out in her mind and urged her to finish what she'd started. And the voice had a point. Why else had Ellie driven all the way back to Phoenix, only to think better of it and stop at that swap meet instead of the airport? Why else had she gotten that gun before driving back to Robert's house? Why—

Ellie snaps her face toward her bed. Moving away from the door, she carefully closes it and backtracks to where the green vegan purse lies on the duvet. Breathing shallowly now as her heart thumps against her breastbone, she sits on the mattress and unsnaps the bag's front flap. Looks inside the main compartment to see her essentials along with the nonessentials that she dumped in from her other purse — old lipsticks, concert ticket stubs, crunched-up receipts stuck to lozenges, crushed water bottle, dried-up pen, and a balled-up scarf, of all things, to wear in this summer heat. And then she remembers and blinks once. Snaps the flap closed and eases a hand into the special front side pocket instead.

Empty.

Ellie swallows, tries to choke some air down her dry throat.

No gun.

Never had been.

But that's what she thought, what she's known all along. Hasn't she? How could she not? She'd bloody well remember if she bought a fucking firearm.

She hadn't even bought the purse for that purpose anyway. She just liked it. Something that caught her eye. Something different, something cheap. She only noticed the CONCEALED CARRY sign after the fact, thought it was absurd but darkly funny. So American.

And that was it. Curiosity had diverted her on her way to the airport, and retail therapy was enough to raise her spirits and change her mind about leaving. She would return to Sedona, to Robert's marital home, and speak with him civilly. End it on her terms.

So, then, how did that voice...

How had it distorted her reality so thoroughly? So vividly, so believably? Because there *was* a voice, wasn't there? She didn't imagine that, too?

Christ, I've gone mad. Ab-so-lute-ly crackers.

Still, though, she needs her sodding car keys. Or maybe the rental place will pick her up, if she explains so very nicely? Not without a not-so-very-nice fee, she's sure. Well, however she has to manage it, she'll get the bloody hell out of Dodge, or whatever the Yanks call it. This red-rocked, white-washed theme park attraction has officially worn out its welcome in her life.

She's staged her British Invasion, and now it's time to retreat.

I almost wish now that she did it. That she would, and just blame me and get away scot-free.

But what does that achieve, really? Would it make any difference? Is that the resolution we want? The revolution?

No. At least, I don't think so.

And anyway, if she did point the finger at me, she'd get nowhere. Without evidence, without me, *it wouldn't even amount to so much as "she said–she said," her word against mine.*

She said–she's dead, more like.

B-Side

Waiting at the window, keeping an eye on the rest of the world going by, Ellie takes her time to regroup, feeling no need to hurry. What's there to rush to anyway?

Yet, as the minutes crawl past, this game she and Robert are playing starts to drag her down. Stepping out into the arid air, Ellie quietly shuts the motel door behind her.

She waits for no one.

Robert isn't coming, so she needs to go to him, to his house. She can't navigate herself from here, though, not really sure where *here* is after she was driven away in the night in her stupor. But she does know his address.

Right. Off to Robert's monstrosity of a house, then. His monstrosity of a marriage. Get it done and dusted.

This place is the vortex of hell, and I'm leaving before it sucks me in.

A sudden wave of dizziness overtakes her just now. Still standing beneath the motel's overhang, Ellie backs up against her door to steady herself. She realizes she hasn't eaten since Phoenix, that she drank her dinner last night, and is severely dehydrated.

That would explain a lot, *actually.*

She ought to find some sustenance. The good doctor probably isn't home now anyway, and when she really thinks about it, she can't stomach seeing him yet. Besides, he wouldn't just keep the keys from her; he probably *is* on his way here, and—fine. He can just pop the keys into reception, then. Ellie's getting the hell away for now.

She breathes to clear her dizzy mind and quell her fussy stomach as she steps out from the overhang and feels the morning heat on her face. Exhaling, she strides past her abandoned rental car and cuts across the lot to the street.

Wandering along the sidewalk, she hopes for a café somewhere among all the souvenirs, art galleries, tourism businesses, and, *bleeding hell*, all the rock shops. Crystals wink at her from every other window, it seems, and now and then she sees a sign advertising Vortex tours.

Vortex? So I was right! This is *the threshold of hell.*

But as her gaze moves from the rustic strip of stores to the rusted rocks rising in the distance, she eats a bit of crow on that last thought. She's never seen anything like this, doesn't understand why the hills are shaped and colored the way they are. Kind of like how she felt about herself growing up.

Maybe somewhere in that stone is the real reason she's meant to be here. Brought here by something she can't quite yet manifest in her mind, but, in the meantime, those natural platforms and pillars are there to hold her up. Maybe what her imagination took way too far in the motel room was the simple, far less literal message to shed Robert from her skin and seek higher ground.

Fuck's sake, girl. What are these thoughts? Get food and fluid in you—NOW.

She's never been one for morning meals; a biscuit and espresso are enough to coast on until poorly improvised elevenses at Ink & Intuition, scrounged up from the back cupboard for a late-morning snack. Nothing gets her stomach prowling for its prey, though, like a spicy homemade dinner, and now Robert's ruined even that.

No mind. She's ravenous, ready to pick up a new habit: breakfast. A platter of huevos rancheros, carafe of water, and one bloody big Bloody Mary later, Ellie collapses back in her heavy wooden chair and smiles almost orgasmically to herself. She could get used to this daylight eating. Amazing how a re-plenished body can overhaul your entire perspective. Or maybe it's just the vodka.

Whatever it is, Ellie feels charged and ready to head back out into a day that has nothing to do with Robert at all. The instant she's back on the pavement and out in the exhilarating heat—which feels so good pressing into her skin after sitting in the restaurant's frigid air-con—she homes in on that red rock again, and the vibrant blue sky beams her in.

A hike. She should go on a hike. Robert told her they would, so she packed all the right kit for it. She doesn't feel like going back to the motel to change, though. Not yet. She's only just feeling better, more like herself, and unexpectedly eager to paint her own colors all over this grand canvas. The hike would be a perfect way to do it, but going back to that room…back to the "body"…to the everything that never was…

She isn't ready. Isn't prepared to find out if that voice, that vision, hadn't just been her imagination. In the incredible case that it was real, she's got to exorcise it somehow.

Shopping it is, then.

Ambling up the road, the souvenir shops call her in one by one. But she doesn't buy anything. Nothing speaks to her, and the teenaged clerk at the last store reminded her of a younger Robert, like it could be his son, which is entirely possible and sets her mind whirling again. She succumbs, and into the void she goes, where not even the blindingly beautiful sunlight can reach her. She feels acutely alone. A drifter, an outsider, all by herself with nowhere and no one to go to for thousands of miles. So far from where she belongs.

Because she *does* belong somewhere, if not here. Doesn't she?

Ellie looks around at the pedestrians along the street. Most of them probably aren't from here either. She isn't the only one, nor is she the only one alone. Even those accompanied by others look so solitary, focused on their phones and not speaking to each other as they forage for virtual company instead. All the lonely people…

Ellie's experienced it both ways, the loneliness when not alone and then when very much alone. The isolation when minds and hearts were closed to her before actual doors closed on a face no one would ever see again.

So, yes, there was a time she *didn't* belong anywhere. But now she does. In London. At her parlor, among her friends and clients. And no matter what now, no matter where, she belongs in her skin. That's what she loves so much about her work, her way of helping others present who they really are, too. Nowhere does she feel more at home than on her stool next to that chair at Ink & Intuition.

Something's displacing her at the moment, though, and no wonder. Never mind being alone in a foreign country; it's this landscape. This place couldn't be more unlike where's she's from, like she's landed on Mars and the red planet's already been colonized—and franchised, except McDonald's golden arches are turquoise instead. Familiar yet different. Everything.

No, it's nothing like where she's from, but what does that even mean? To be *from* somewhere, and why does it matter? *Where do we all* really *come from anyway? Where do we all belong?*

Ellie turns her head to the distant rockface now fully illuminated in sunshine, and her body follows accordingly as she takes her next step.

She doesn't make it to the rocky plateau. Hiking still isn't an option, dressed as she is in a maxi skirt and sandals, but she feels her energy grow and grow the closer and closer she draws to the stone. And though the cliffs are still a distance away, she finds her tracks stopping dead in front of a plum-painted building, where her body positively hums.

In passing the shop, she now stands rooted beside it, staring up at a massive mural of swirling psychedelic colors. All shades of the rainbow pulse out in jagged yet hazy concentric circles, like a stone—or stoner—has been tossed in a pond of cosmic energy, rippling the life force with kinetic calm and crazy at once.

A tie-dyed solar system of good vibes and higher consciousness, all rotating around a glittering blue-white, crystalline being at the center. Angel or ancestor, deity or demon, the message is: *Welcome. You belong.*

Ellie's encountered a lot of this stuff in London, yet never to this scale. The side she faces is a decent width and stands two stories tall with a gabled roof. When she backtracks to the lot to find the front entrance, she notices for the first time how long the building extends, like its own little strip mall, but it seems to be all the same business.

THE MEDITATION STATION, reads a weathered wooden panel overhead. Similar vintage-style signs with inverted corners line the building's upper paneling, advertising CRYSTALS, BOOKS, TAROT READINGS, PSYCHIC READINGS, CLASSES, and VORTEX TOURS. Tugging the central door open to the sound of twinkling little bells, Ellie steps into a crystal cavern of incense-rich air.

The mystical strum and twang of a sitar cascades over her ears and plucks at the strings of her psyche. She associates this sound with so much; it's the soundtrack of her childhood, of visiting grandparents in northern India, of recitals and celebrations at temple. Of a sitarist in a restaurant garden, who once let her awkwardly hold the long instrument and place her little spindly fingers anywhere but on the right strings.

Memories move through her of an enchanted and curious time, a spell only broken by the adults who perpetually stood around her as she aged, filling her head with only the things they could see. Rigidly spinning her into the image of what they thought she was supposed to be—until they screwed her into the ground, stable but stuck. Unable to grow in her own direction or pull free from her roots.

Until she did.

Now, deliberately or not, she rarely hears the sitar. Not unless Morcheeba or some such fusion band cycles through Ink & Intuition's speakers. The sound and scent of *this* place, though, is so tangible, its atmosphere so thick, Ellie thinks she might choke on it.

Breathing through the filter of her fingers, she inspects the picture wall in the foyer as an excuse to linger near the door. Actually, she *is* intrigued with the three rows of photos covering the wall. Headshots, a dozen and a half of them. Why?

In the dim light, she scans the faces. Most are white and nondescript, middle-aged on average, she'd guess, and mainly captioned with women's names. They all look kind but unremarkable — until Ellie's gaze falls on a pair of striking eyes. Set within skin a shade darker than Ellie's, they're penetrating, entrancing, even, and Ellie can't distinguish pupil from iris in the low-res image.

"Are you interested in seeing one of our psychics?" a yellow-blond woman asks from a counter a few meters from where Ellie's standing.

Caught with her hand still covering her nostrils, Ellie fakes a runny nose.

"Oh, ah…" She glances back at the eyes that had her so transfixed. "No. No, thank you. I'm just having a look."

The middle-aged woman at the counter smiles warmly from within her sun-spotted, crow-footed skin. "Far out. I'll just leave you to go with your flow. But if you need anything, I'm here." Turquoise pendants and beads clack together on the woman's neck and wrists as she nods her head and gestures around the store.

Her sunny smile does draw Ellie in, away from the dark hall of photographs and into a bright LED-lit lair of shiny, happy, earthy everything. Infinite points of amethyst twinkle from both small and tall fairy caves scattered around the space.

Moseying along, Ellie's foot bumps into a basket of raw, grubby-looking yellow-brown crystals marked with a sign saying NATURAL CITRINE. On the shelves are glossier, sculpted and polished stones in the form of skulls, spheres, and pyramids, among other shapes. Along one wall, the crystal spectrum is organized in rainbow order for chakra healing. Ellie turns her attention to an adjacent room. Tarot cards, oracle cards, Lenormand cards, runes. Floor-to-ceiling bookshelves are stuffed with them, along with guidebooks on divination and all things esoteric. On her way in, she also spots a poster explaining Sedona's "vortexes" — spiraling centers of energy that make the area a spiritual hotspot.

In other words, "hellmouth." As I thought.

Perusing the little room, Ellie is delighted to find a tattoo-themed deck. She lifts it from the batik-clothed display table and turns it over in her hands, nodding in approval of the artwork on the box. Reading the description at the back, she likes the concept of tattoos as a way of inking fate into your skin. Ellie sets the deck down. Picks it back up. Shakes the box and likes the rattle of the cards inside. She rocks out to the rhythm of it for a while.

"We've got decks for twenty percent off right now," comes a dulcet voice from behind Ellie that scares the ever-living hell out of her. Perhaps this is the salesperson's polite way of telling her to knock off playing with merchandise if she doesn't intend to buy it. "Not that one," the same blonde from the counter says as she steps around to Ellie's side, "but if it's calling to you, I can make an exception." She winks.

Ellie smiles and turns the box side to side in a show of indecision. "I don't really know how to use these."

"Aw, it's simple." The saleswoman waves a hand, her tone genuinely encouraging, not hard-selling. "You just gotta leggo the ego and let the soul speak, y'know?" Her gaze glides along Ellie's bare arms and breastbone. "I really dig that one." She motions with her finger along the length of Ellie's forearm without touching it.

The art nouveau lily that Ellie has planted there is actually her favorite. She smiles broadly. "Thank you."

The woman does touch her hand to Ellie's arm now, just a tap, like she's flirting. "Unreal with your complexion. Where ya from?"

"England. Visiting from London."

"O-oh."

Ellie can tell from the two-syllabled tone that she hasn't adequately answered the question. But if the woman wants to know where Ellie's "really" from, she's received nothing less than an honest answer. Pressing her lips into a tight grin, Ellie sets the tarot box down on the blue batik.

"UK, wow." The sales associate gives a little chuckle. "So, Beatles or Rolling Stones?"

"Pardon?"

"Which one?"

"Do I prefer?"

The woman excitedly bobs her head, probably a staunch fan of both.

"Is it all right if I say neither?"

"Oh." The tanned woman reddens. "For sure. I just assumed…"

A lot of things. And yet.

Ellie shrugs. "I do live off Abbey Road," she adds to meet her halfway, "so I could possibly be swayed to that side."

Before either of them can say anything else, a man's voice booms through the shop.

"If anyone's interested in a psychic reading, we have ladies waiting upstairs."

Ellie pinches her brow. Between the headshots in the entryway and "ladies waiting upstairs," this place has certainly taken on a brothel-like quality. She snorts at the thought and then wipes her non-running nose when the saleswoman looks at her. "Allergies."

"Tell me about it. You'd think a desert would spare ya, but even just the dust…"

Ellie bites the inside of her mouth and nods.

"That deck is totally you, though," the lady continues. "If you're drawn to it, remember, I'll give you a special discount."

"Oh, cheers, but—"

"Or if you wanna learn the tarot, you might try a reading with one of our professionals."

"Right."

Ellie looks over the woman's leather-fringed shoulder to scan the store beyond, as if the colorful crystals over there are twinkling Morse code at her to get out while she still can. Those lovely stones, hacked off Mother Earth and tumbled and chiseled and dyed into whatever people want them to be, hoping they'll do all the healing for them. The psychics aren't the only ones being pimped here.

Her gaze falls on that basket filled with nubby, grubby, diarrhea-colored citrine. The real deal, not the bright yellow-orange, heat-treated stuff that she saw advertised for the solar plexus chakra.

"Excuse me," Ellie says as she brushes past the likewise yellow-orange, heat-treated blonde.

Ellie steps up to the basket and squats beside it. Doesn't love the unregulated "market" price for a rock, yet runs her fingers along the rough points anyway. Feels a twinge when her hand passes over one. Picks it up. Grips it in her palm as a honeyed heat swells within her center, just below her breasts. She lowers her eyelids and sees a warm glow appear behind them as her snake-ringed thumb rubs the rung-like ridges of what feels made for her hand. Or what her hand was made to hold. This smoky, unadulterated citrine that would somehow help her find light in the void.

With it in hand, Ellie stands and pivots toward the checkout counter. "I'll take this," she calls over to the saleswoman, who's still standing by the tarot table, arranging her wares. "And that deck I was looking at." She points at it with the citrine, as long as the woman's standing there and can grab the box.

The woman sweeps over with jewelry jangling and fringe flapping and appears to quite happily ring up Ellie's items at the till. She notes the special twenty-percent discount once again, and while she takes her time manually doing the sums with a calculator, Ellie's mind drifts from the tarot cards on the counter to the psychics upstairs. Waiting. She half expects one to run down any second now, just as she's about to leave the store — because wouldn't a psychic have predicted Ellie's visit? Sensed her downstairs? Doesn't any one of them have an urgent message of love to send Ellie from Robert? A sign of what the bloody hell she should do next?

Much as she's taking the piss right now, damn it if Ellie hasn't just tempted herself. What if there really is something to all of this? To that inked paper, to these mined stones. She picks the citrine up from the glass countertop and eyes all the glistening crystal rings, pendants, and pendulums encased below. She's seen those conical pendulums before, knows they're used like dowsing rods to find answers, and she wonders if she can't find an answer right within her raw little crystal. She closes her eyes, takes a deep inhale — smelling that incense for sure, but also the dried sage stick smoldering at the end of the counter — and silently asks her sweet citrine what she should do.

The glowing ball of solar light drops from between her breasts to right into her gut. *Yes.* Someone's waiting for her upstairs. The one from the photo. The one with the eyes.

She hears the store associate bag her cards and then opens her eyes to see her reach for the receipt. Just as the woman tears off the printed strip of paper, Ellie asks, "Actually, ah, might I do a reading as well? Tarot?"

The blonde widens her cigarette-stained smile and pumps her head up and down. "Far out!"

Winding up the creaky wooden staircase, Ellie finds herself in a musty-scented hallway. Through the dimness, she makes out the second door on the left, the one she's been sent to after requesting her specific psychic medium.

Stepping up to the door, she leans against the opposite wall, waiting to be summoned. The dark hall has a murky blue tone, and the thin carpet beneath her feet looks kind of cruddy. The door before her is nothing special, blank as she feels, and she becomes more convinced by the minute that no answers unlocking the universe's mysteries will be found behind that piece of plywood.

Until it opens. And Ellie is greeted by the brightest of smiles beneath the darkest of eyes.

"Hi, I'm Beverley," comes a rich, silky voice.

Mirrors to my soul comes to Ellie's mind when she looks into those big brown, almost black, irises. The thought's from out of nowhere, yet she believes it. Or wants to. She guesses she'll find out soon enough.

"Come on inside," Beverley says as she creaks the door back farther, opening the way for Ellie to enter the candlelit room. "You can have a seat just there."

She motions to an empty chair pulled away from a small table. On the other side is what must be Beverley's seat, with a thick-knit, Southwestern, cream-and-black cardigan draped on its back. Spread across the table itself is a deep wine-colored dupioni cloth, embroidered with a golden mandala design and topped with a few crystals, tealights, and pillar candles on either side. Strung from the walls are more batik textiles, along with tribal patterns, feathers, and macramé hangings.

Shapes and patterns dance in the candlelight, and Ellie notices the incense isn't so strong in here. It smells more like sweet sage and fresh linen, soothing her more than anything has in recent memory. Sitting as Beverley instructed, Ellie slings her flea-market purse onto the chair back and tucks her recent purchase into the hanging bag. She takes an opportunity to close her eyes and inhale the calming essence while the psychic shuts the door to the hall.

"So, you're Eleanor," Beverley's lush yet soft voice almost purrs as she assumes her own seat. She has a slight Southern lilt and appears to be around Ellie's age—late twenties, maybe early thirties.

"I am." Ellie smiles.

She envies how Beverley keeps her dark afro curls natural, grown out into a bouncy burst around her heart-shaped face and falling just below the chin. Ellie enjoys her own thick hair, but she'd easily trade her long, wiry waves for that kind of effortless volume. Maybe she could cut and style her hair in the not-so-effortless way. She's been thinking of going back to brunette, too. But before her mind can race through any more of these superficial thoughts, Beverley tips her head and fixes Ellie with a contemplative stare.

"You weren't always, though. 'Eleanor.' You went by something else, I mean."

Ellie feels her smile drop. *Please. Don't.*

"Sorry." Beverley lowers her head and shakes it, tapping her forehead with the tip of her middle finger.

"Occupational hazard?" Ellie offers to smooth over their mutual unease. Is this psychic for real? Sensing dead people and deadnames alike? Ellie's not sure she wants to find out. Didn't ask for it.

"Um, yes. You could say." Dimples pierce Beverley's cheeks as she grins, though her eyes still apologize. "But you're here for a tarot reading. That's what you've paid for. I just need to confirm that."

Ellie nods.

"Okay, then, though I *am* a medium, I'm not channeling anyone for the next thirty minutes. Just so that's clear."

Ellie nods again.

"Unless you want to?" Beverley's gaze darts all around Ellie. "Is there some—"

With her chin tipped toward her chest, Ellie flitters her head side to side.

"Okay. So, they're *here*"—Beverley circles a palm toward Ellie—"but I won't be communicating with them."

Ellie just stares.

"Sorry," Beverley repeats. "I just need to be sure. A lot of folks do expect more than they pay for as long as they're here and I'm able. Which I don't mind. Truly. It's my gift to give, but if the schedule's tight—" Ellie must be giving a wary look, because Beverley hastily adds, "Look, I'm not trying to sucker you into upgrading your session. I mean—"

With her eyes rolled to the ceiling and hands fanning in expressive circles, it's like Beverley's attempting to dial that back. Her genuine fluster immediately endears Ellie to her. The way her movements bounce her breasts around in her blouse is pleasing as well. Ellie wonders if those are natural, too, and feels envious again.

"Of course, no worries," she's quick to assure Beverley. "I understand. But yes, just the tarot reading, please."

"Okay." Beverley exhales, with another self-deprecating eye roll. "Good." Then, with that brilliant smile, she claps her palms together. "Let's get started."

"Right," Ellie whispers, in part to herself because she's suddenly excited about the prospect of this, whatever *this* is, yet nervous over what else the psychic medium might sense about her, intentionally or not.

"Have you ever had a reading before?"

Ellie shakes her head. "I work near a shop that does them, but if I'm honest, I don't know how much I believe in all this, type of…" She gestures to the table and around the room.

"Woo?" Beverley stretches her peach-glossed lips into a side-smile.

"Well, yeah." Ellie politely smiles back. "All due respect to what you were able—to, what you said, before. But—"

Before Ellie can remotely articulate a complete sentence, Beverley reaches across the burgundy silk with palms upheld, inviting Ellie to place her hands in them.

Ellie hesitates but does so. Feeling Beverley's thumbs press gently against the fine bones of her hands, she meets her intense gaze as Beverley says, "I won't violate your mind like that again. Not without permission. I really am sorry."

Ellie's been storing her breath in her chest for the last several seconds, but now she lets it eek out, a bit at a time. "Thank you," is all she says, eager to just get the reading underway.

Beverley starts with a cursory explanation of the process, insisting that while certain tarot spread positions can indicate a future outcome, "We are the deciders of our own fates. The outcome can always be changed—if we will it and do the work."

Then, she lights a few sage leaves with one of her candles and leaves the herb to smolder in a little brown ceramic dish. Fanning the smoke across the table with one hand, Beverley reaches behind her with the other and grabs a card deck from a low bookshelf. Holding the deck above the sage for a moment, she lets the smoke waft over it before setting the stack of cards on the cloth with a satisfying thud. She asks Ellie to shuffle them, to infuse them with her energy.

As she does, Ellie catches a glimpse of the artwork, certain she recognizes the deck. "I think I just bought this one," she says as she shuffles.

"Thought so."

"Because you read my mind?"

Beverley smiles with a *give-me-some-credit* gleam in her eyes. "Because your shopping bag is see-through." Crossing her arms, she sits back with a smug grin. "I noticed when you first walked in. Thought you might like to give 'em a test drive."

Ellie grins back. "Cheers." After giving the cards one last good shuffle, she knocks on the deck with her knuckles three times as directed before Beverly next asks for her birthdate.

"Fifth August," Ellie says before she can correct herself, watching the other woman flip the deck face-up and thumb through it.

"Ah. A Leo," Beverley says, casting an eye on Ellie, who knows she's really a Pisces. If the psychic detects the lie, though, she doesn't call it out, simply plucks a card from the pile and lays it on the cloth for Ellie to see. "Here's our gal. She represents *you* in this reading. Your significator. And let me tell you, she is something fierce."

"I'd say so," Ellie agrees as she hovers over the image, getting a closer look in the dim, flickering light and admiring the fiery hotness of the Queen of Wands, whose golden mane is like

Ellie's, just glossier. Also like Ellie is the tattoo on the queen's soft-looking skin; her dark, defined brows; and full, luscious lips. This queen's eyes are blue, but damn if they don't match Ellie's determination.

"Then we do have a fit." Beverley smiles. "There are other court cards of different suits in the deck, but this one in particular reflects a creative, passionate, driven individual. She's confident, sensual, and feels good in her skin."

Just as she starts to feel a fire welling within, Ellie's dowsed in cold water at Beverley's next question. Which is, simply, what *Ellie's* question is—for the cards.

She draws a blank. Question? She didn't think she needed one. Her only question now is what's her question?

"Personal? Professional?" Beverley prompts, which sends Ellie's mind whirring. The parlor's business has been solid lately and their newest artist only exceeding expectations. Ellie feels good there. But personally...

Bollocks. Where to even start? Ellie isn't sure anymore if she wants to talk about Robert, and like hell if she's going to bring up what she experienced at the motel. As hard as she tries to consider other topics, however, Robert keeps returning to the forefront—the image of him, anyway, lying bloodied on the floor. All she wants all of a sudden is to see him, be sure he's really okay. And if so, to just...leave things on a better note than they did. Does Robert want that, too? After dumping her off last night, does he have any intention to return? Does he want anything to do with her? Does she want him to want to?

Stewing in discomfort and indecision, Ellie returns her roving eyes to Beverley when the psychic leans forward onto her elbows and laces her fingers together. The polish on her long nails matches her lipstick.

"Is it about the guy you just saw again? Is that the one?"

The one, as if Beverley could see the flurry of questions swarming Ellie's head and seized on "the one" that kept pushing its way to the surface.

"Yes," Ellie says before she can think about it. "Yes," she repeats in lieu of further detail.

"Thought so," is Beverley's only comment before giving the tarot cards a quick overhand shuffle and asking Ellie to cut the deck. Ellie does, and Beverley pulls three cards from the top of the re-stacked pile. "Huh."

Laid before Ellie are deep jewel-toned drawings rendered in the style of tattoo art, their rich color and symbolism popping out from a vintage cream background. Reading from left to right, the cards' captions say *Judgement*, *The World*, and *The Emperor*.

"All Major Arcana," Beverley says. "That's significant. The Minors deal in day-to-day stuff, but the Majors are more ongoing, overarching issues, you know?"

"Okay," Ellie says with furrowed brow, studying the pictures but unable to make meaning from them. Other than that, in profile, the brunet Emperor kind of reminds her of an unshaven Robert — what *isn't* reminding her of him today? — and that the religious overtone of Judgement — depicting an angel blowing a trumpet above people rising from graves — puts her ill at ease.

"This is big-picture stuff. In your relationships, romantic or platonic, you've grappled with the judgment of others and yourself. Most recently, you might've done something you're not proud of, behaved in a way that let you down when you know you're better than that. Were you too harsh on this guy? Channeling how others have treated you, maybe? Quick to label and cut off?"

Ellie sucks on her lower lip.

"Don't beat yourself up over it. See that?" Beverley taps on a woman who's standing up from inside her coffin. "It's like you've had a rebirth. Just learn from missteps and heed your soul's call, which in the present seems fulfilled. You may not fully realize it, but you *have* achieved completion when it comes to your heart. Look at how free this woman is," she says, pointing to the World card now, "naked but not vulnerable. She, too, is comfortable in her skin and just owns it.

"Nothing is finished forever. Life's a turntable, and you'll cycle through insecurity and heartache again, as we all do, like a record spinning round and round, skippin' on the same scratches. But each time, your needle wears down those imperfections more and more."

Ellie automatically thinks of her tattoo needle, how the concentration and repetition of her craft ever more effectively imprints everyone she serves with a piece of her, living on in new flesh.

"With enlightenment, you're bringing something finer and fiercer to the table, Queen of Wands. You're in command of your fate here, and it seems by putting yourself out there in a truly vulnerable and authentic way, you really have managed to find the real deal. This man, he's showing up here, in your future." She points to the Emperor. "He might seem all powerful and patriarchal on his throne, but see how he's looking at you. He's facing the first two cards—looking back at where you've been and where you are—and seems to glow from your radiance. This guy's besotted. Even your queen here"—she points to the significator card—"is looking down at him like *da-amn*. She wants him, and she's holding that wand, that tool for directing her power, willing it to do her bidding. You're in more control here than you think."

Ellie's been listening attentively up to this point—rapt, in fact—but the morning's big breakfast and Bloody Mary are catching up with her. She yawns before she can help it.

Beverley stops mid-soliloquy. "Oh, *I'm* sorry. Am I *boring* you?" She only manages the straight face for so long, laughing robustly at her own act. Ellie is so enamored with the good-natured sound and smile that she reciprocates.

"Listen," Beverley continues, "I don't know who we're talking about here, what's happened between you two—like, *really* happened, not what's in your head." She's no longer looking at Ellie but the space between them, her eyes appearing unfocused. "But you've got something there that isn't over yet. I'm seeing unfinished business, heat that needs releasing to find closure. Someone needs to move on."

"Someone?" Ellie asks. "As in me? I need to confront him and get over it?"

A sound catches in Beverley's throat, and she swallows. Her eyes meet Ellie's, slightly widened. If it weren't so cliché—and truly creepy to contemplate—Ellie would think the psychic has just seen a ghost.

"You?" Beverley says at last. "No, no. You both."

Her voice is as distant as her stare, but even in the candlelight, Ellie sees the light come back into her eyes. Beverley clears her throat.

"You and the—the guy," she says, as if Ellie couldn't already figure that out. "And even though you're still seeking *that* completion, with him, what will help you find it is your current state of wholeness. You're embodying who you are. You don't need this man to be complete. But he's a key factor somehow in a new cycle you're starting. Maybe more conventional than expected, but not like what you've left. He offers a healthy stability, in which you'd continue to flourish. He wouldn't—" She blinks her eyes, which have become glassy, and shakes her head. "He wouldn't treat you as less-than. He only sees you for who you are, and…

"And I'm jealous as fuck." Beverley chuckles toward her chest and wipes her eyes. "I'm sorry." She looks up, her expression almost sad if it didn't also look a little scared. "I don't mean to monologue at you. That's just what I see, in this moment, so why don't you take it from here. Tell me what did or didn't land with you."

In all the time she's been listening, Ellie would swear she stopped breathing if not for the shallow inhales of sage-spiced air that she's felt caressing her nose. She feels light, dizzy but light, and morbidly relieved to hear Robert still spoken of in present tense. Yes, she needs to see him again. But for now, how much should she tell Beverley?

She decides to tell it all. At least, up to the part when she first discovered Robert was married, and then attempted to hightail it back to London via Phoenix. The coming-back-to-Sedona part is still a little fuzzy for her.

"I'm not normally this daft," Ellie says quietly at the end of her story.

"None of us think we are, until love comes along—or what we think is love. Then we're absolute fools for it." Beverley laughs down toward her lap again, albeit bitterly.

Ellie wonders what experience the psychic is speaking from but is sure Beverley doesn't want to make this session about her. Ellie has to forge ahead with her own history.

"I thought he was the proverbial 'different.' The one who finally saw me for who I am, not who I was assigned to be." She gazes at the soft halo of a candle's flame. "But now you've just said that, which would mean I read him right, and...I don't know how to process that with everything that's happened since. I don't, I don't know if I can believe him again. Or in *this*."

She motions to the cards, feeling prickly and petulant all of a sudden. Looking down at her lap, she traces the pattern on her skirt with a fingernail, her jaw clenching.

In the upper periphery of her vision, she sees Beverley sit back. "I understand," the psychic says. She must get this all the time—people who come to *her*, asking for her service, willing to pay for it, and then resenting her when she tells them what they don't want to hear. Except in this case, she's said everything Ellie could've hoped for. So what else was she expecting? Wanting? Maybe she's just pissed that Robert got more validation than her anger. The good guy she shouldn't be so tough on. Poor wittle Wobert. The cards said nothing of his dishonesty, so what's the deal with that?

When Ellie looks up, Beverley's gaze is grazing her arms and chest with interest. "Your tattoos must tell you stories all the time. Maybe even change their tunes depending on the day."

Ellie tilts her head, considering that.

"Our minds instinctively read meaning in symbols," Beverley goes on. "We can't help it. We look at pictures through our unique lenses, and what we see reflected back are answers we already possess. On some level, consciously or not. Tarot is a useful tool for drawing that out, not telling us what we want to hear but what we need to see.

"But this is a snapshot. A bird's-eye view. We can go deeper if you want, to get into the nitty-gritty of other influences at play here, like what really brought you to my table today. Let's not forget, Eleanor, that I do bring more to a reading than just intuition and a knack for storytelling. I'm not channeling anyone—not deliberately—but I am tapping into our shared, higher consciousness to help interpret some of these meanings on your behalf. It's up to you, though, if any of this resonates."

Ellie feels bad now for challenging the psychic's trade, provided on Ellie's own request. Beverley's handled it more graciously than she had to, and Ellie genuinely doesn't think this bold, beautiful woman is a charlatan. And yet…

She wants to test her. It's mean, it's what everyone must do, but it's what Ellie's going to do, too. With all the concentration she can muster, she focuses her thoughts on the motel. Her room there. And the vision she had inside of it.

After a prolonged staring contest, Beverley seems to indicate with a small tip of her head that she knows what's up. *All right*, her eyes say. *I'll play.*

"Are you giving me permission?" she asks, to which Ellie nods her consent. "Which motel is it, then, if you don't mind me asking?" She narrows an eye. "Do you feel safe there?"

Oh. Wow. "Uh. Yes. It's fine. Decent. The one just up the road here? The Roche?" Ellie doesn't know why she's beginning to vocalize her answers as questions, just that her confidence is rattled by Beverley's insight so far.

"The Roche Motel." Beverley leans back in her seat again, nodding slowly, knowingly. "Okay. And that's where you last saw him? Last night? Not this morning, like you thought?"

A pressure bears down on Ellie's chest, and she finds she has to work harder to draw sufficient air in. The psychic's clearly lifted whatever veil held her back before and is homing in. Ellie nods just as slowly as Beverley did — but ever so much less knowingly. "Last night."

"But you did see him this morning, like a hallucination? I'm not clear. What do *you* think happened?"

"I think…I don't know what that was. All I do know is that yesterday sent me spinning, and instead of fleeing the country, I came back and confronted him, but not before getting properly pissed on tequila at the first taqueria I saw in town." Margaritas, which she'd never tried before, turned into straight shots with a little encouragement from other tourists, and then — bam.

"I found my way back to Robert's by some miracle — or curse — breathed fire until the whole atmosphere burned around us, at which point he saw fit to collect my unhinged, sorry remains of self and drop me at the Roche Motel. Room paid for in advance, if I can remember that much. And then a hired car promptly whisked him away with my sodding car keys."

Ellie mutters obscenities under her breath at the memory of *that* logistical nuisance.

"Which brings me to this wretched morning," she says, "when I woke with a thumping headache, empty stomach, new vegan holster" — she lifts her purse from where it hangs on her chair — "and a dash of wishful thinking, which must have brought on a psychic break indulging a sick fantasy I never actually had."

"It wasn't that."

That's all Beverley says.

"Well, all the same, I probably ought to consult a medical professional, don't you think?"

"Wouldn't help."

"Why not?"

"Eleanor…"

"You can call me Ellie."

"Ellie." Beverley flashes her lovely pearl teeth before the misgiving reenters her lovely onyx eyes. Picking up the remaining pile of cards, she does another quick overhand shuffle before setting the deck down in front of Ellie and spreading it out, facedown, in a long line. "Mind drawing another one?"

"All right." Scanning the fan of cards, Ellie instinctively zeroes in on one and pulls it out to present it to Beverley.

Ace of Wands, its caption reads. Ellie sees a disembodied hand holding a wand like her Queen of Wands. This wand projects so much more energy, though, as if channeling the very power of the sun's rays. And though the tattooed hand that holds it seems feminine and similar to the Queen of Wands's, on some intuitive level, even Ellie knows it isn't. It doesn't belong to her—the queen *or* Ellie. Someone else is conducting this mad music, changing Ellie's life with a wave of her hand.

Watching Beverley inspect the card for some time in silence, Ellie senses a big *So, here's the thing* coming. She doesn't know why, she doesn't understand how, but true to expectations, Beverley finally opens her mouth to say, "I don't know quite how to broach this delicately, so I'll just come right out and say, well, suggest…"

Ellie tips her chin down into her neck, her raised brow encouraging Beverley to out with it.

"It's just that, our time, for the tarot reading, is up. And I don't care what you have and haven't paid for, Ellie. If I had the time today, I would ask you to stay a while longer, free of charge. But since I don't, and you might not anyway—" she pauses for an inhale, though she herself seems to loathe the unnecessary drama that adds "—Ellie, would you please consider scheduling another session with me? For a medium reading. Tomorrow. As soon as possible?"

A-Side

Back at the Roche Motel that afternoon, Ellie verifies at reception that Robert indeed prepaid for her room — and for the entire week. So, he evidently doesn't want her staying at his house, but he doesn't want her to leave town yet either.

She supposes she could be flattered by that — hopeful, even — or at least appreciative that he took her flight itinerary into consideration, in case she does want to stay. Yet, though she resents him doing anything on her behalf — she can take care of herself and will mail him his money back — this whole mess *is* decidedly his fault.

She's surprised to learn, however, that he never stopped by, at the very least to drop off her car keys. He didn't even leave a message with the front desk. Well, no wonder. For all Ellie can't recall of last night, she does know she spewed some truly cruel, drunkenly horrendous words and told him in no uncertain terms to fuck off forever. Even if he doesn't take that seriously, the man just probably needs a day.

Closing the door behind her, Ellie looks around at her room, wondering what could be so sinister that it even had Beverley on edge. Well. Of course she knows what. But she's still inclined to believe it's more about herself than this place. The fuckloads of trauma she's endured in life, brought to the boil by this latest betrayal. That's all — surely?

Otherwise, this is just a room, probably identical to every other room down the line. By the light of day, it amuses her. The rugged wood, leather, "native" patterns and paintings, furry hides, and horned skulls all scream a theme, and she contemplates what's appropriate versus appropriated. It does create a warm, cozy aesthetic, though, charged with masculine energy yet speaking to an ancient, intuitive feminine essence somehow. The overall effect is an androgynous, shamanic vibe that hums out from the walls.

Rather than let the atmosphere ripple over her, Ellie mundanely slides the beige Kokopelli curtains across the window and drops her purse on the bed with a sigh. She sits next to it on the mattress and kicks her sandals off, then falls back with another heavy exhale.

Reaching into the plastic shopping bag for her natural citrine, her hand brushes against the box of tarot cards. She sits up and pulls both items from the sack and uses the crystal to help cut open the deck's plastic packaging. She thumbs through the cards, their meanings lost on her until she finds the Queen of Wands and counts down to the Ace of the same suit, the one setting fire to the whole sequence.

Laying every card down but this one, Ellie reclines back again, considering the Ace in her hand and thinking about what Beverley said. About giving the good doctor another chance. Even if it was just to hear his side, she could then be well and done with it.

She couldn't remember much of what was said between them at his house, just that it had escalated quickly and she'd done most of the yelling. Closing her eyes now, she recalls hearing Robert's repeated pleas to let him explain, that he didn't expect his wife would be there, that he'd tried calling Ellie's mobile, but she must've had it turned off, sending him straight to voicemail. She hasn't thought to check that yet. Her mobile phone's been off since boarding the plane at Heathrow to avoid roaming charges. She could've gotten an international calling plan but assumed she wouldn't need one when the only person she wanted to speak with, be with, was Robert. She figured she could use his phone if she had to anyway.

Ellie opens her eyes and rolls her head to stare at her purse. Reaches over to fish out her mobile. She clicks it on, glad to see there's enough battery power left to search for a signal. Charges be damned. She needs to know.

Dialing her voicemail and then pressing the cool crystal screen to her ear, she listens to the polite automated voice listing her menu options. Ellie hesitates only for a moment before tapping *1* with her thumb.

It's Robert. She hears the nervous edge in his voice. But he's trying to remain calm, she can tell, just casually requesting she postpone her arrival that day, making it sound like it's a work thing but he'll explain everything when she gets there. His sign-off is distant but overall normal. The next message is also him. Not as calm. He's speaking low, though not quite whispering, and doesn't mask his urgency. Not only must they meet at a later time, but somewhere else as well. Not the house. A restaurant. He's sure she must be peckish if not famished after her long journey. Several more messages are from him, too.

Ending the call, Ellie sees the emails and texts that have simultaneously flooded in. The vast majority from a certain Dr. Robert Rigby. All with the same message and increasing panic.

Right. So, he was scared shitless and trying to warn her but still not forthcoming with the truth. A truth he hadn't been ready to share with her in London, she understands, but something he should have—and *could* have—told her. She wouldn't have faulted him the way she does now.

She flicks the phone away and hears it skid against her faux croc bag. Tapping her fingertips on her stomach, she closes her eyes again. *"I didn't know she'd be here,"* says his voice in her mind. *"She just showed up."* Little by little, the fragments of last night piece together, and in between Ellie's accusations and choice expletives, she hears Robert saying something about property, that she—the other *she*—had come for some of her things. And the house. They're selling the house. *She* wants an independent appraiser and has her own agent. *Blah-blah* about *she-she*—the cold, stainless steel logistics that bury the emotions of a relationship when its body's barely cold. He didn't even call her by name.

Ellie can imagine what he's going through, feels sorry for him, even. But he still should've told her. And she can still let him tell her, in the way that he tried to when she wouldn't listen. She *will* let him. Yet whatever love she may have felt for him, she can only believe it's dead now.

Warm tears stream off her face and seep into her hairline and ears. The hangover coma Ellie started to slip into earlier is returning, and she feels the pinpricks of sleep sparkle over her limbs. She hopes she hasn't hurt Beverley's feelings by turning down a follow-up session. She just needs to sort this herself. Just needs to rest…and then she'll sort it…once she wakes up.

The Ace of Wands is still in Ellie's hand as a purplish black fog rolls in and over her consciousness. And then it all begins to fade until it all becomes clear again.

I'm still here. And I will be there.

I am everywhere now, Eleanor. And our business isn't done. Because I don't believe your love for him is dead, that it's not behind those tears you pretend to cry for no one. Even when you know what you know. You're living in a dream. You know what they're like and that he'll be no different, given enough time.

You no longer need him. But I need you. And I think you need me. We'll do it right this time. We'll be reborn. And then neither of us will need anyone else ever again.

The blast of a gunshot jolts Ellie awake. The motel room is notably darker. Even through the closed curtain, she can tell it's night.

Someone is speaking, whispering, but she's not hearing it with her ears.

Please...don't wake me to this again. Leave me as I am.

The voice does go quiet as Ellie implores it to, but a presence lingers.

You're not real, Ellie insists as she rolls to her side and pulls the covers up to her chin, heart racing. She squeezes her eyes closed. *I'm only sleeping.*

Yet the sense of someone else in the room has her slowly raising her eyelids again. The room is dark, and as she looks around, she sees that, in the center of it, down on the floor, something is even darker.

I'm only sleeping. It's just a dream.

A shadow, a form, lies sprawled on the ground. And hovering above it is a grey mist, which pulsates and writhes for a few seconds before dissipating into nothing.

The shadow, too, fades into the carpet.

Ellie blinks. Rolls onto her back. And just lies there. Staring at the ceiling, waiting—hoping—for sleep to return, if she isn't already asleep and imagining all of this.

But then her stomach stirs. And she knows she has to get up. That she's slept away the day and needs to eat something before she can sleep again.

And come morning, she knows what else she must do.

B-Side

A new day breaks, and Ellie's mind is aching when she wakes in the middle of a dream. She's had the deepest sleep of her life and is still yawning by the time she's up and ready for a hike — finally. She might be crazy, but she needn't be lazy. So she heads for the hills, bowled over by their beauty even more at close range and in the early morning light. With the fresh air and sun shining down, she feels good, like her feet barely touch the ground.

She's in a whole new state of mind when she returns to the motel room. Her black trainers are now dusted with reddish-brown dirt, a souvenir from the trail to go with the small rocks she collected in her pockets along the way — some rusty, some tan, and some a deep, sparkly blue. She even got pricked by her first cactus, which still stings so sweetly.

Stripping down, she steps into the bathtub and welcomes the shower's spray. She lathers up and exalts in the feel of her own curves as she massages the sudsy soap down, down, down. Ellie loves this body. Not exactly the one she was born with, but the one she was born to have. And she does have it. It's hers. It's *her*.

Robert loved her body, too. The way he explored and caressed and kissed it was almost prayerful. She could've wept at the respect he showed it, that he showed *her* — with the exception of his critical omission, of course. But he hadn't faked the rest, and he'd known her truth, yet now she has to question if it was all just some kind of game for him. Had he just fetishized her, or is Robert really the evolved man she'd fallen for? The one Beverley saw in the cards?

Enough. She's whole without him, just like Beverley said as well, and she doesn't need his validation to reclaim that power and move on. She has another matter to tend to now, a bizarre one that actually does lie beyond her control. She still doesn't understand it, but somehow, overnight, she knows that only one person can help her. And it's not Robert.

Swiftly, Ellie eases into a loose white linen tank top and blue paisley harem trousers, slipping on the same metallic gold sandals as yesterday. She has a class to catch at the Meditation Station, as a pretense for checking Beverley's availability there. Plus, it might calm Ellie enough to cope with what comes next. With her hair tossed into a loose bun, the moment she steps out of the motel room, she feels lighter.

Twenty minutes later, she's barefooted and cross-legged on a yoga mat, eyes closed and ears open to the transcendental music floating through the room. Trickling water, flutes, and birdsong meld and flow with other synthesized sounds as the instructor's soft, soothing voice guides her students to turn off their minds, lay down all thoughts.

"Relax and feel yourself float downstream…surrender…"

Ellie's busy mind initially finds it difficult to not hop onto every train of thought like a stowaway keen to ride anywhere. Her knees feel tight, her foot's falling asleep, she keeps thinking about thinking, and this teacher could be tripping on acid from some of the surreal things she says.

Yet eventually, the inner noise does quiet down, and Ellie becomes weightless, floating and surrendering to the void of her mindscape, which appears black as the cosmos until it glows purple, then red, then orange, and then a whole spectrum of visions, everything shining, knowing, being. After a time, she can almost *hear* the color of these abstract daydreams, and before she knows it, she's gradually guided back to Earth, twitching and flexing one body part at a time to ground herself back in her skin.

Well, she certainly does feel more relaxed—and visualized some amazing new tattoo concepts. Now, she just needs to inquire about Beverley.

Sandals back on her feet and purse strap clutched within a nervous fist, Ellie ventures into the shop section of the complex. She meets Beverley's disarming eyes as she passes by the entryway photos, and the incense almost needs a machete to hack through on her way to the counter. As she waits for someone to attend to her, she hears the spilling strains of a sitar again, accompanied by traditional *tabla* percussion. And vocals—in English.

This is contemporary Western pop, drawing on Hindustani classical music. As Ellie looks upward at the intangible audio, trying to make out why the voice sounds so familiar, an orange-and-blue being enters her peripheral vision.

"I knew it. Team Beatles," says the sun-seared blonde from last time, sporting an acid-wash denim jacket.

"Oh, is *that* who this is?" Ellie asks, knowing she recognized those vocals for a reason. With a band as ubiquitous as the Fab Four, she doesn't have to love them to know them, as if the human brain automatically downloads their discography at birth.

"We're playing 'em all day. Getting psyched for the *Yellow Submarine* screening this week. Fiftieth anniversary!"

Ellie actually knows about this. Having started—and apparently ended—their relationship at her Abbey Road address, Robert teasingly threatened over email to drag her to the *Yellow Submarine* sing-along this Thursday, joking it was why he'd picked this specific week to invite her out. The Sedona International Film Festival had already hosted the four-part *Deconstructing the Beatles* docuseries late last month, soon after Robert returned from London. Seeing it advertised everywhere, he just *had* to attend it to nurse his homesickness for her. Or so he said.

Anyway, the thought of this sing-along gives Ellie hives. She does fancy the song that's playing now, though. "Which one is this?" she asks, pointing a finger at the ceiling as though a speaker were right there.

"'Love You To.' George Harrison was very inspired by Indian music." In emphasizing *Indian*, she raises her brows and nods at Ellie as though this factoid surely appeals to her ethnic background—when, for all the woman knows, Ellie could be Bangladeshi.

Ellie simply smiles and says, "Far out."

"Ellie," Beverley greets at her darkened doorway. "I'm glad you decided to come back."

"Well…" Ellie stalls for an excuse as she resumes her seat at the table. When she finally got back to business with the sales associate downstairs, she was in luck that Beverley had an open appointment just fifteen minutes from then. Ellie opted to wait upstairs in the hall, rather than browse the store and see how many more prejudice points the associate could score.

The same candles are lit on Beverley's table, though the pillars are noticeably melted down, their wax building on hammered brass plates below.

"How'd that go for you?" Beverley asks after Ellie finally mentions her meditation class.

"Soothing—and psychedelic!" She laughs, recalling the color swirl of images in her mind's deeper dimension, where galaxies curled around her like a hug and dragons carried her out to sea. Even circles and triangles somehow had four sides. "I think that teacher fancies herself the Dalai Lama, chanting from a hilltop. But it was brilliant."

"I'm glad. Did it help?" Beverley asks pointedly.

"Okay," Ellie concedes, "so maybe meditation or even medicine wouldn't be enough for my situation. What happened at the motel, I mean. It's unnerving that my mind could go somewhere so dark, so fast. And I had another hallucination last night."

"The same?"

"No, at least I don't think so. Not as defined. And it was apart from me. But the rage was there, the revenge. I don't know. I just knew I needed to come back here. To find you. You're the one who'll bring us peace."

"Us?"

A breath catches in Ellie's throat. "Me."

"Maybe Robert, too?"

"I guess."

"Or the other one."

"I don't—"

"I think you might."

The women hold a long stare between them. Ellie looks straight into Beverley's beguiling eyes but is aware of the beautiful gold and emerald hues farther below. Her gaze drops to where candlelight dances along the psychic's necklaces, and when Ellie meets her eyes again, Beverley's gaze has deepened; Ellie can almost feel it penetrating above her brow, seeing third eye to third eye, violating yet stimulating. She lets her in.

After the protracted pause, Beverley speaks again.

"I think…maybe…we should take this back to your room."

"What about your other appointments?" Ellie asks as she walks side by side with Beverley along the street. The hot sun blazes the trail before them, yet Ellie still can't see where all this is heading. Just that it's what she's wanted since she woke in another dewy sweat this morning, and clearly Beverley wants it, too.

"They'll get reassigned or rescheduled. This is more important, Eleanor."

"After you," Ellie says once she's swung open her motel room's heavy door. "Home sweet home-away-from-home. Courtesy of the doctor."

Beverley strolls in with a mild smile on her face as she looks around. "I like what you haven't done with the place. Very cliché chic."

Ellie snorts and tosses her room key and bag on the desk, while Beverley just stands in place in the middle of the room, holding her purse. It's like she's listening to something Ellie cannot hear, seeing the unseen. The medium lays a hand on her heart and breathes deeply.

"Someone's here," she says softly. "But she's hiding. Hesitant."

"She?"

Beverley nods.

"Who?"

She shakes her head. "Don't know yet."

Closing her eyes for a few beats, she reopens them, staring ahead of her.

"She's already stronger, though, than when we first walked in. I think she feeds off you. Your energy. She relates to it, taps into it." As her gaze seems to lose focus, she inhales another deep breath. "I think she's trying to draw on my energy, too. I sense her emerging now, but only tentatively."

"What now?" Ellie asks, and Beverley closes her eyes again.

"We wait."

"For what?"

"Not sure."

"All right. So," Ellie ventures, "what do we do, exactly, while we wait? Do you need me in here? Or do you work better alone? Shall I leave?"

Slowly raising her eyelids, Beverley fixes Ellie with another sidelong gaze. A smirk curls the corner of her lips before she speaks again.

"Wanna get high?"

Twenty minutes later, the two women are down on the floor, reclining on every patterned pillow and scratchy, woolly throw to be had in the room, with a few vending machine snacks littered between them from a preemptive run. No attack of the munchies yet, but good to be ready, just in case. Plus, they stocked Butterfinger, Beverley's favorite.

Sunlight streams in through the narrow gap between curtains. Lying on their backs, the women watch its beam crawl across the ceiling and walls.

"Mmm," Ellie exhales, two streams of smoke speeding from her nostrils. She's holding her citrine point in one hand, and with the other, she lifts the tightly rolled joint up to her line of sight. "I have *got* to get you into my life," she tells it.

Beverley rolls onto her side, propping her head up with her hand. "Have you smoked pot before?"

"Not like this." Ellie continues giving the joint loving googly eyes from beneath ever-lowering lids as she passes it back to Beverley. With her thumb, she languidly strokes the ridges barcoded onto her crystal, like she's scanning for data, the histories and mysteries encrypted in the earth. Then she stares at the ceiling, waiting for a sleepy feeling to take her miles away.

Instead, she feels a door open at the stem of her brain, which unleashes all manner of thoughts that never quite complete themselves. It unsettles her stomach, and she rests both hands on her soft belly as she turns her head to face the psychic. "Anything?"

Beverley takes a slow drag and then blows rings toward Ellie's face. Closing her eyes, Ellie breathes them in.

"Sometimes it helps," she hears Beverley say, "and sometimes it hinders. I thought in this case it might open me to her more. Invite her out."

"Is she still here?"

"Yeah."

"But not from here. Right? If she stayed at this motel?"

"Not sure. But she definitely died here. She's giving me that much. That she's connected to this place, not you—in case you're worried something's followed you."

Ellie's not, but she isn't ready to wrap her mind around a ghost haunting this motel either, even though she's the one who brought Beverley here to suss out that very situation. The psychic would've had more business at the shop; she certainly didn't need to clear her schedule for one gig. Unless she charges top dollar for house calls.

"Why are *you* here?" Ellie pivots onto her side, mirroring Beverley as she props her head up, too.

The other woman chuckles and, dropping her head back, she rests her hand on the shapely curve of her hip. "Here in this room or this place in general?"

Ellie did mean the former but replies, "Both."

Beverley lifts her head to face Ellie. "Well, I'm *here* now because I want to help. Free of charge, by the way."

"No, no, I don't expect—"

"Listen. Back at the shop, I could pick up what your spirit guides told me secondhand, but it's stronger at the source. I think this is serious, and I want to hear it from the whore's mouth." Her eyes immediately go wide, and she covers her mouth as she's lost to a fit of giggles. "*Horse!* Horse's mouth!" Dropping her head back again, she howls with laughter. "This stuff *is* good, isn't it?"

Ellie pinches her brow yet laughs along in the haze of her own giddy high. "Can't say I'm familiar with the expression either way." Surmising her new friend has probably had enough for a spell, she reaches to slip the smoking joint from Beverley's hand, bringing it back to her own lips. "Though in this case, I might prefer communing with a horse. Less frightening."

"Don't fear her," Beverley says, strikingly somber relative to a moment ago. "She was the victim here."

"Of what?"

After a deep exhale, Beverley stares off and shakes her head. "Something violent. Violating." There's a slight tremor in the muscles around her mouth as she says it.

"Was she shot?" Ellie whispers.

Beverley looks down at the floor then off to the side, toward where her purse lies just beyond her elbow. She shakes her head again. "No. But I think she wishes she was."

"I don't understand. What happened to her?"

Still zoning out, Beverley only sighs. Ellie isn't sure if she can't say or won't say what the victim in this room endured. If the medium is unable to see it clearly or wants to spare her pro bono client some sordid details.

Trusting she'll tell her more when it matters, Ellie rides the wave of her streaming thoughts in another direction. "So, what brought you *here?*" This time, she swirls the joint in the air to indicate the greater locale. "Arizona."

Blinking rapidly and seeming to snap back from wherever else she was just now, Beverley says, "You don't think I'm from here?"

"Is anyone?"

Beverley shrugs. "Someone must be. But as I'm sure you've noticed, there's not a lotta brown in this town."

She laughs richly again as Ellie protests that that's not what she meant, that it's the woman's subtle drawl that made her curious. If Brits are expert at anything, it's dialect. Speak one sentence back home, and people can practically identify what street you were born on.

"Georgia," Beverley states with a straighter face. "All my family's back there. But I... Two years back. I left." Freed of the weed, her fingers tap on her upper thigh, just where the hem of her denim mini skirt meets her deep, smooth skin.

"On your own?" Ellie realizes she knows nothing about this woman she's already started to consider a friend — if she has a partner, kids, pronouns, anything.

"Yeah," she replies before briskly reclaiming the joint from Ellie's fingers. She shifts her bottom out from beneath her to lie on her back again, and her gaze leaves Ellie, shutting her out as she puffs more smoke from the rolled paper. "And you, Khaleesi? You from the UK?"

Ellie nods, although no one — except maybe a ghost, apparently — is looking at her to see it. "I live in London."

Still facing away, Beverley asks, "And were you born there, or —"

"I'm from England," Ellie snaps instinctively. That gets Beverley to look at her.

"Yeah, so I figured," she says with eyebrows raised. "I just wondered if you grew up in the city itself or somewhere outside."

"Right." Embarrassed, Ellie tries to laugh off her twitchy trigger finger.

But Beverley puts her at ease when she rolls back onto her side to face her and says, "I get it. Sometimes I'm asked where my parents are 'really' from. And the answer they're lookin' for isn't Georgia."

The two lock eyes and smile.

"I'm *from* Lancashire," Ellie says, "in northwest England. I left when I was eighteen."

"You were unhappy there?"

Oh, I see. She can ask follow-up questions but dodges them herself?

Yet Ellie obliges, unafraid to share a past that the psychic's already gleaned to an extent. She slides her thumbnail along the crystal's ridges. "When I was a 'boy,' everything was all right. For everyone else, anyway. So I wore the face awhile. But who was it for? Not me."

"So you left it all behind."

"Buried along with the name. Nobody came after me."

"Somebody did." Beverley's dilated pupils are trained on her.

Ellie shares a soft smile as she admits that truth with a nod. "Eventually. Secretly."

Beverley squints. "A sister?"

"Practically. My cousin." Ellie's heart swells at the familiar face in her mind. "I owe her so much. Her and some tremendous friends."

"For helping you become?"

Ellie shakes her head. "Just letting me be."

She takes the stubby, smoldering length of rolled paper, purses her lips around it, and sucks the last hit before stubbing it out in a shallow piece of pottery she'd brought over from the desk.

"Look, Beverley, I'm ready to leave this place behind, too. But if I check out of here, whose problem is it next? Has this happened before, and will it happen again? Could someone get hurt? *Has* someone? What does she say?"

In the span of Ellie's words, Beverley's eyes have emptied again, her lips parted and appearing to form around silent words. Eventually, the veil seems to lift, and she says, "I want to tell you."

"Okay. Then please do. By all means."

The medium squeezes her eyes closed. "I'm…hung up on…I don't know. So many words…filling my head with things to say, but then…they slip away. With *you* here. Because it's not only me…not *my* mind confusing things, it's…"

"Shall I make myself scarce? If I'm interfering with your signal or whatnot?"

But Beverley doesn't reply. Just lies back on her short stack of pillows, dropping heavily onto them with her eyes still closed.

Ellie worries the medium has strained herself too much with the psychic effort, blames herself for getting Beverley in the middle of this.

Whatever the hell "this" is.

She decides she's okay to stay until Beverley says otherwise. Laying her head on a pillow, too, she just watches her breathe.

When the other woman remains unresponsive to the awkward silence that's fallen, Ellie wants to glide her hand over Beverley's curls, to caress and comfort her the way Ellie's closest cousin would, when she used to babysit Ellie and listen to all her troubles, big and small. But she doesn't, knowing enough self-entitled folks have probably helped themselves to Beverley's hair over the years. Instead, Ellie gently strokes the woman's cheek with her gaze, for whatever solace it might offer her psychically.

After a time, Beverley's heavy lids lift, her eyes blacker than ever with their enlarged pupils.

Ellie can no longer deny there's something here, in this room, and it's come between them. Someone is speaking—to Beverley this time—but she doesn't know who's there.

Looking and yet not looking at Ellie through her darkened eyes, Beverley startles her by taking Ellie's hand and cupping it over her breast. Ellie is confused, wants to yank her hand back, and yet she leaves it, if only to confirm whether those baps are natural or not. The question's admittedly nagged at her, and the psychic must've picked up on that, wants to satisfy the curiosity that's had Ellie eyeing her curves since yesterday's tarot reading. It's a well-meaning but unfortunate habit; Ellie genuinely doesn't mean to ogle, knowing how much she herself resents an uninvited gaze.

Even now, though, she impulsively indulges the distraction, loving the feel of real breasts when hormones weren't enough to make her own the size she wanted. Her cousin used to let her touch hers, too, when visiting from uni while Ellie was a young teen. It was just fun, a way for girls to bond. Ellie means nothing more by it, but isn't so sure now about Beverley, who seems to exalt in the touch as she stretches an arm above her head and curls it around her bottom pillow.

Ellie twitches her face away when the woman, moments later, moves in for a kiss. She drops her hand and sits up. "I'm sorry."

Beverley eases herself up, too, into a crouch, gripping her purse as she shakily straightens her legs to stand. Ellie didn't even notice her pick the bag up, though supposes she's been rather distracted in the last minute.

"I'm sorry," Ellie repeats from where she still sits on the floor, staring up at the other woman, who's no longer looking at her but the door.

"I want you out of here," the psychic says, clutching her bag closer to her with both hands. "Now."

"Okay," Ellie replies, wide-eyed, getting to her feet, too. "I'll just pop out and—"

Her back is turned to Beverley, in reaching for the room key on the desk, when Ellie hears a click behind her. Looking around, she drops the key to the floor at the sight of a revolver, aimed straight at her.

"Beverley?" she barely squeaks out. The air's been sucked from her chest.

"You shouldn't have come," the other woman says, voice shaking and accent altered.

"As I said, I'll go—"

Ellie is backing up toward the door when Beverley brings her other hand up to cup the one holding the gun. Ellie stops in place.

"Where the fuck did that come from?" Ellie's terrified that she's seeing her vision made manifest, that from the ether could come a physical threat, locked and loaded. Or is this another hallucination? Have she and Beverley been brought into the same dream? Or is this only hers, Ellie's, under the influence of the pot or spirit or both? Is her life not actually at risk?

It feels real enough when her hesitation allows Beverley to advance across the room and press the gun's barrel against her breastbone.

"Why?" Ellie whispers.

Beverley's lips tremble, her eyes watering. She's near enough—and close enough in height—for Ellie to see herself reflected in those giant pupils. They mirror her just like she thought at the shop. But these can't be windows into her own soul. Ellie would never do something like this, would never want to.

Except for when she did. Lost to delusion.

Fucking hell.

"Beverley," she says sternly. She's become mildly aware that she's still holding the crystal, as if it's adhered itself to her hand, and she squeezes it for strength. "Snap out of this. You've gone under her thrall."

Tears stream down the other woman's face, and Ellie sees the misgiving in her eyes, but those eyes still aren't Beverley's.

"Stop this," Ellie tries again. She feels a golden glow grow in her center and radiate outward. Smoky letters begin to form in her mind, drifting then congealing into something more defined that she can pluck out of the void. "Please...*Anna.*"

"I warned you to go away, to leave me alone. Go harass someone else." She presses the barrel harder into Ellie's sternum. "And you probably did, didn't you?"

"*Stop.*"

"But I won't let you harm another woman. Never again. *You're* the whore, you bastard, and you've fucked your last piece of meat."

She pulls the trigger.

Recoils.

Shakes the revolver out of her hand and drops to her knees, sobbing.

Ellie drops to her knees as well. Presses her palms against her chest as she rocks to and fro, heaving air in and out.

The gun wasn't loaded.

But the accusations were.

"What the ever-living *fuck*, Beverley? Anna? What happened to you?"

The other woman's face is pressed to the tatty carpet, her wet makeup rubbing into its scruff as she hyperventilates against it. Ellie reflexively leans in to lay a hand on her shoulder, but Beverley twitches away and scrambles back to their mess of pillows and snacks on the floor. Drawing her knees up to her chin, she cries into her hands.

Ellie, meanwhile, seizes the chance to snatch up the revolver and stow it in the nightstand drawer, next to a Gideon Bible. On her feet, she crosses to the window next, sets the citrine gently on the desk, and throws open the curtains to let the sun shine in. Then, slowly, she crouches back to the floor and crawls to where Beverley sits, hoping the woman — either woman — will let her in.

Beverley crosses her arms above her knees, wipes her nose on her wrist, and finally looks up. Her pupils have contracted, and she looks more like herself, despite the smeared mascara. Ellie reaches out to wipe the blackened tears from her eyes.

"I don't know what to say," Beverley murmurs.

"It wasn't you." Ellie wipes the hair from her eyes next.

"Wasn't it?" Beverley sniffs, then rubs her nose on her thumb.

"I guess I don't know. You tell me. What happened?"

Another sniff, and then Beverley responds, "She didn't mean to do it. Not to you. Her sorrow and regret, piled onto mine, it's—" she swallows "—it's almost too much to handle."

Staring off to the side, Beverley releases her arm from where it was folded under the other and scratches her head just above the ear. Ellie hears the woman's stomach growl, so she fishes a Butterfinger from their stash on the carpet and offers it in a sign of peace.

Removing her hand from where it disappeared into her hair, Beverley manages to breathe out a light laugh and say, "Thanks," as she takes the candy. She opens the wrapper but seems to have no appetite for the chocolate, just stares at it and frowns like the mere sight of it tastes bitter.

"What are you doing with a gun?" Ellie asks, shuddering as the reality of its *realness* washes over her.

The wrist holding up the candy bar goes limp. "It's never loaded, but I—just need it near me. To feel safe."

"From who? Someone in particular?"

Beverley nods and inhales deeply. "The bastard I left in Georgia."

"Was he violent?"

Beverley diverts her eyes as she nods once more. She seems to subconsciously rub her fingers above her ear again, still holding the candy with her thumb. "Took me for everything I had, too."

"Con artist?"

"Tax accountant."

Ellie grimaces, wondering which is worse. And then Beverley tells her the tale of how the nefarious taxman had seduced his way into her affections and then weaseled his way into her business. She'd recently moved down to Savannah from Atlanta and opened her own psychic boutique there, complete with a wide range of witchcraft and wellness products that earned her a pretty penny. At least enough to live on, and she was satisfied with that until Taxman took over and told her how it was going to be, that from here on out she was working for no one but him—not herself, not anymore. And that she'd better not try any of her "voodoo" on him, because he'd know and then he'd kill her.

Whenever she tried to stand up for herself, tell him he could do what he would with the store but he didn't get to hang a sign on her—*wham.* The lights would go out and she'd see stars. The final straw was when he struck her with one of her own crystal balls. On the side of her head, right above the ear.

She left without a trace and with a restraining order. And then she bought the gun. For two years since, she's lived in constant fear of him showing up at her home, at her work. Not a day goes by when she doesn't see his face on the street, out a window. When she isn't flinching, tensing, preparing. To get through it, she just tries to trust in herself, in her power to protect and predict, which, thank God, her head injury didn't hinder.

She just never thought her gift would one day be used against her.

"She was so challenging to access," the psychic says of the spirit now, "so reticent and reluctant. Then all of a sudden, the door just opened and—*whoosh!*" The candy wrapper crackles as she waves her hand. "Bye-bye, Beverley, hello—"

"Anna." Ellie speaks the name that appeared to her mind before, just like the birthdate had even before that.

"You know," Beverley says, her head tipped a little, "*everyone* has psychic abilities. Some access them more easily than others, but"—she points her Butterfinger at Ellie—"I'd say you're more attuned than you've probably realized."

"Me?"

"I think that's why I see you as clearly as I do. Like the window isn't open, but the shade's up. And I suspected as much when you lied to me about your birthdate yesterday." Appearing to feel better as she sits up with more energy, Beverley finally bites off a good chunk of her candy bar. "You were born in February, am I right, Pisces?" she asks with her mouth full. "*Her* birthday was August fifth."

"In sixty-six," Ellie says before she's barely thought it.

Beverley bobs her head. "That's the year. She was almost your same age, though. When she died."

"And how did she? Did she shoot someone? Then kill herself?" Ellie swallows. "Can you tell me?"

Lowering her knees to sit cross-legged, Beverley requests that Ellie do the same before taking each of her hands in hers to form a circle with their arms.

"She'll show you."

A-Side

A knock on the door.

It opens to a dim sky and smug grin. He stands there — until he doesn't. Slips past. Invites himself in where he's not welcome.

Beer and tequila on his breath. From earlier — a dinner. Business, not pleasure. Our group went and stayed out. I didn't. He's disappointed. Came to find me.

I don't want what he wants, didn't send the signals he saw. My resistance disappoints and delights him. He calls me a prude and a whore.

The struggle excites him. Escalates. A slap and a sting. Wood floorboards rushing to my face. His hand pinning me by the throat. Head throbs and veins pulse as grip tightens. The floor tilts one way and then another. Arms I think are mine fight like hell until they blur above me. Movement slows as mind dizzies. Throat closes as fingers tighten.

He gets his way. With something, not someone. The thing on the floor that's become less me. Is becoming even less.

Me, who pulls farther and farther away, slipping, slipping, free and fast. Into the quiet, into the blank. Doesn't even know he's killing me until he comes and I go.

"He was her boss," Ellie says, opening her eyes to the magic circle she formed with Beverley. "She died while he, when he was…" She squeezes Beverley's narrow hands.

With tears returned to her eyes, Beverley nods, the tale obviously taking its toll on her the second time around, too.

"Here." Ellie scans the carpet where they're sitting, the hard floor it's concealing. Her face breaks into a silent ugly cry. "She relates to both of us," she says as Beverley cries with her. "So much."

Her animosity toward Robert aside, Ellie wishes she didn't relate to the physical violence Anna and Beverley suffered as well. The sad truth is, not every man has reacted like Robert on hearing her backstory. So she knows the feel of a fist, of hair yanked from the root.

"That's why her will was so much stronger with both of us in here," Beverley says.

"Enough for you to carry it out. Really carry it out. Not a vision like I had with Robert. She had you aim a real gun at a real person. Me." Breaking off, Ellie sobs, her palms pressed against her eyes. "But why?" she squeaks. "Why me?"

"I'm sorry." Beverley breaks down for a moment, too. "So sorry. I hate what I did. But you have to believe it wasn't really me, Ellie. I swear. I couldn't even see you anymore." She scoots in and wraps an arm around her. "She wasn't seeing you either. Only him. All these years, with nothing to do but relive that night and imagine how it could've gone differently, wonder if she could still make things different. It's like she played the scene over from the start, this time going along with his intentions and seducing him so she could distract him and go for the gun. She knew I had it."

"Right. Him." Ellie's nose runs as more tears fall. She huffs in a few quick breaths as anxiety seizes her chest. "A scenario reimagined, in which *you* aim at *me*. When it bloody well could have gone the other way round."

"What are you saying?" Beverley drops her arm from Ellie's shoulder as she leans away and gapes at her. "You wish you got a shot at me instead?"

Beverley's brow is furrowed, but she slowly raises it with dawning comprehension of what Ellie's getting at.

"Oh my God, Eleanor, no, no, no." She wraps both arms around her now, pulling her into a tight hug. "She sees your soul, don't you understand? She sees it like I can, and you're Eleanor. That's all we see when we look at you—*you* you, not what others saw with only their eyes. It has nothing to do with that."

Ellie continues crying into Beverley's shoulder, but her breathing calms as she listens.

"I'd say it had nothing to do with you at all," Beverley adds, "that she cast us the way she did because I had the weapon and you were another warm body, but I think she did target you specially. For different reasons than you think. She's lonely, Eleanor. I sense she hoped to keep you here as a companion, and maybe me, too, if I couldn't live with what I'd done. And that way we'd be spared future hurt at the hands of men, too. It's *so* outrageous, I know, but who's she got right now but us? The ones who probably get her the most? Who hear her voice?"

Beverley's speculations are jarring, yet Ellie's breathing continues to slow. She wants to hate Anna if any of that is true, that taking Ellie's—and maybe Beverley's—life could be any remedy to her own being cut short.

Yet as Beverley herself said, Ellie does believe she has her own psychic sensitivities. Because right now she feels the immense remorse that Beverley talked about. The perpetual pain and confusion that torments Anna, only compounded by the grief of what she just did. What she *nearly* did. The blood she almost had on her decayed hands.

"Honestly," Beverley says, sniffing and wiping away the remnants of her tears as she sits back from Ellie, "I don't think that gal knows *what* in hell she wants. She died traumatically over twenty years ago and has been tortured ever since, through no fault of her own. And the violence inflicted on her…it's like he filled her in with all his sins, too. Reason and what's right get twisted in that vortex of anguish, until even the well-meaning become misguided, paving that way to hell with 'good' intentions. We think everyone learns all the answers after we die, that if we're a person of peace we'll rest *in* peace, but it's sadly not every soul's journey. Not right away."

Ellie lightly, pensively, scrapes the corners of her mouth with her thumb and middle finger, staring at the carpet. "What now, then? How can we bring her peace when we haven't made our own? She's the real Queen of Wands, and all we did was fan her flames, consuming ourselves in them." *No one here was saved.*

Beverley hangs her head and drifts it side to side. "I don't think so." Looking back up at Ellie, she narrows her eyes, as if reading her again closely. "You and me, we're okay. We might not think we are, but let's be real. On some level, we both know we are, right? We're gonna be fine because we saved ourselves before and we'll do it again. As for her…"

She looks off to the side, as though listening for something. "She's retreating again, and I doubt she'll come back all guns blazing next time. Her energy's spent, for one, but I think she's also had a chance to see it wouldn't give her what she needs. Her existence — she doesn't really want that for us. It's like she's been caught in a revolving door, spinning and spinning, but we're what it took to break the cycle. Maybe. Hopefully. I don't know. These things can take time."

Before Beverley can say more, a strong knock sounds on the door.

She and Ellie look at each other, tensed. Ellie points her chin at the nightstand, indicating for Beverley to retrieve her empty gun, just for effect, just in case. Ellie herself wipes the moisture from her face, stands, and walks to the door, grabbing her citrine from the desk for a little added courage. Glancing at Beverley, who gives a nod, she gingerly turns the knob and pulls the heavy door open.

Outside in the bright light stands a petite woman of middle age. With straight, light brown hair pulled back in a loose po-nytail, she squints at Ellie with a friendly smile. Her sea-green eyes look tired but kind.

She introduces herself as the motel's owner. She lives just beyond the family-run business and is here most days — was working the front desk this afternoon, in fact, when a Dr. Rigby dropped off a set of keys.

Ellie accepts them from her. Notices an extra keyring attached. With a plain key, not the transponder ones for the rental car. Instinctively, she knows it's to Robert's house. He's letting her know where he stands so she can choose for herself. Stay or go on her own terms. No pressure from him.

"Did he leave any message?"

Smiling sweetly, the woman politely says no and asks if there's anything else she can do before one of her employees takes over for the evening shift.

"Actually," Beverley chimes in from the nightstand, where she left the revolver alone, "if you have the time, ma'am, there's something we should speak to you about."

B-Side

"Thanks for seeing me off. Sorry you gotta haul to International now."

"Honestly, I don't mind. I've got time."

"All right —" Beverley leans in for a one-armed hug "— then I'll let you be on your way. Safe travels back."

"Cheers. You as well," Ellie says, her green croc bag and suitcase in hand.

They stand outside the queue for security at one of Sky Harbor's domestic terminals. After spending one more night in Sedona — on Beverley's sofa bed — Ellie flies back to London today. She knows she's ready to leave. So the two friends drove her rental car to Phoenix this morning, where Ellie's dropped it off and Beverley's also catching a last-minute flight.

Ellie still hasn't spoken to Robert, but she wears his key on a chain around her neck. It does mean something to her, even if it's to a house going on the market soon. She knows she can unlock more than that if she wants to. That's enough to bring her peace for now.

Otherwise, if she stays, she's afraid she'll never want to leave, and that's not what's best. For either of them. He has a divorce to finalize, and she has a life to lead. When he's got his shit together, he knows where to find her. And then...

Maybe.

Beverley, too, is finding her harmony with a short trip home. She's taking that midnight train to Georgia—not to be in *his* world, oh *hell* no, but to reclaim the magic of her own. She's scared, but the whole experience with Anna has encouraged her to escape her own cycle of fear before it spins her out of control of her own life. She misses her family, her friends, her favorite haunts. She wants to see them, and that's that.

Neither woman wants to abandon Anna, of course. She's just taking time off as well to reenergize. They've made the Roche Motel's owner aware of the situation, meanwhile, and the woman wasn't altogether surprised. She remembers the case about the young Chicago consultant who came here on business and, after a dinner meeting, was assaulted by a company executive; she believes the assailant is still serving his time for the rape and manslaughter.

Beverley has asked to return to the Roche once she's back from her travels. She's happy to render her services free of charge, will do whatever it takes to help Anna cross over. All she asks is that Room 7 remain unoccupied, just in the near future. In the meantime, the three women pray for Anna's soul in their own ways, making certain she knows that while she couldn't save herself or those abused before her, her death did ensure that man never laid hands on a woman again.

"Oh," Beverley says. "Almost forgot." Digging in her back pocket, she pulls out two tarot cards. "I know you've got the deck, but I thought you might like to have these extra, to carry with you, use as bookmarks, whatever." She chuckles as she hands them to Ellie.

On top, Ellie sees the familiar Queen of Wands, but below her is the King of Cups.

"You do possess her fire," Beverley says. "We didn't get that wrong in the reading. But as a water sign, you'd traditionally be Cups. They represent emotions and intuition, which you have great capacity for, Eleanor."

Looking at the king, Ellie raises an eyebrow, starting to feel troped again.

Beverley shakes her head. "This is about energy. Receptive and expressive. We all have both, our yin and yang. I choose the king for you because you don't just feel, you act. Why the hell else did you come out here, going the distance for Robert? Why'd you come to me, concerned about Anna? Sure, your Wands energy makes you feisty and fickle sometimes, but your Cups energy tempers that. You've been through the wringer, girl, and all things considered, you've shown amazing command and compassion. God's sake, you comforted me after I shot you!"

It's shocking they're able to kid about that now. That they already found it a royal hoot last night over Micheladas and enchiladas. But they need to laugh and are just happy to have something—anything—to laugh about.

Eyes welling, Ellie drops her purse onto her suitcase and draws Beverley into her arms for one last, proper hug. They both squeeze tight and sway side to side.

"Don't get your gun confiscated at security," Ellie murmurs into her hair.

Beverley gives her shoulder a little smack. "Ha, ha."

"But seriously," Ellie says, leaning back to look into those mesmerizing eyes, hoping she'll always be there, reflected in them in some way. "If you need me—with Anna or anything—just ring, my friend, and I'll be round."

"Will do, sweet girl. I'll see you on the flipside."

Single

Six Months Later

Heavy raindrops patter against the window like little drumbeats. The winter day is wet and dreary, but inside Ink & Intuition, all is bright and humming.

Ellie is rendering the final touches of a purple pixie's wing when she hears her name — a colleague asking for her at the front desk once she has the chance.

Wiping excess ink from her client's ankle, Ellie bops her head to the jaunty tune playing through the parlor, the weight of her loose bun bouncing with it. Returning to her delicate detailing of the wing, now and then she hums along with a Matthew Sweet cover of "And Your Bird Can Sing."

"All right, my darling," she says after another minute. "What do you think?"

The university student squeals and even sheds tears of delight. Excitedly flutters her feet, and it's like the violet fairy takes flight. "Aww, she is sooo brilliant. I love her! Thank you!" Stretching to hug Ellie from the chair, the young woman then hops off to admire her new tat in front of the full-length mirror at the back of the shop.

Pleased with yet another satisfied customer, Ellie starts to sanitize her station when she sees movement approach in the corner of her eye.

"He says he's already had a consultation with you?" the guy from reception says from behind a much taller, tanner man.

Staring from where she's bent over her black vinyl chair, mid-wipe, Ellie blinks once. Twice. The blue eyes looking back don't flinch, but they're terrified. Tentative.

She knew in time they'd meet again.

"He doesn't have an appointment," her skinny colleague goes on, "but you do have an opening if you want to—"

When Ellie closes her eyes again, she reopens them with a glare in her receptionist's direction. His pale face goes even whiter.

"Ah. Sorry." He scratches his scruffy mop-top. "Maybe the schedule wasn't updated. I didn't—"

"It's fine." Removing and dropping her disposable gloves into the bin, she straightens to her full height. She still only comes up to Robert's shoulders, but her stance is the more powerful of the two in this moment. Jutting out her chin as she sizes the doctor up, she says, "I can take him."

A gleam enters Robert's eyes that says, *I believe you can.* The playful innuendo in that gaze disarms her a bit at the knees, but she stands strong. They both know she can hold her own. And that she will. With or without him. She's a woman he must believe.

But damn if anyone can succeed like Dr. Robert.

There's so much they have to discuss. And they will. But her heart knows what it wants. This lifetime is short, each day going so fast. Too fast to not seize one before it slips past. To act on what she feels. Love him while she can.

She finishes her cleanup of the last job and sorts the preliminaries of the next one. When Eleanor finally situates Robert in her throne, she takes her seat beside him.

Placing her needle in his groove, they play their song over from the beginning.

"Revolve Her" was written for the limited-edition Paperback Writers *anthology, published in 2019 by Locklear Books. Benefiting the World Literacy Foundation, this multiauthored collaboration was inspired by the music of the Beatles. My story in particular spins song titles and lyrics from the* Revolver *album—with "She Said She Said" (my favorite) as its springboard.*

More

Keynote Speech

Delivered at the 2017 Upstate Eight Literary Festival.
St. Charles North High School,
St. Charles, Illinois

Good morning, everyone! I can't even begin to tell you what an honor it is for me to be here with you all today, in the presence of such talented writers and in the school where I used to teach.

My career path has admittedly been a rather meandering one, but St. Charles North was one of its most important destinations. I owe so much to this place. And to the Upstate Eight overall, as I grew up in Bartlett (go, Hawks!), but since there wasn't a Bartlett High School back in my day, I received my education at Elgin High School (any Maroons here? Go, EHS!).

I'm an old-fart forty-year-old now, but believe me, I remember being your age...the fun and the uncertainty and the whole career path still ahead, not yet sure where it'll begin. Maybe you do know what you want to do, or maybe you're still figuring it out like most folks. Maybe you'll seek publication one day, or maybe writing will remain a happy hobby.

These days, all of you write for class assignments, but, if you're here today, you likely also write privately as a creative outlet. Maybe you submit work to your school's literary magazine, or maybe you write flash fiction or fanfiction online. Or perhaps you just keep it all to yourself in a well-worn and trusted journal. We all write for our own purposes, but the main point is that *we all write*.

When I think about my own writing life, I can't help but look way back to grade school, to the Young Authors contest at Wayne Elementary. I don't like to brag, but…I won that contest when I was in sixth grade. I'd written a gripping coming-of-age tale titled "The Kid Next Door." I not only wrote the story, I illustrated it. Double threat. And after I won, I did a school-wide publicity tour, visiting different classrooms and reading excerpts.

But never fear, it didn't go straight to my head. I didn't start out on top as an eleven-year-old. That wasn't my first go at writing and setting myself up for acceptance or rejection. Oh, no. I had first entered that contest in second grade, when I submitted a short story called "The Panda's Lost Mother." It was a dramatic piece about a *panda* who gets *lost* in the forest. And I gave it this big twist at the end where the *panda* gets *found*. I know. I thought I really had something there.

Needless to say, the story didn't win. Not even close to a runner-up. Because, big surprise, it was a really terrible story. The dialogue was stiff, it told more than it showed, the conflict was severely underdeveloped—and, quite simply, it didn't deserve to win. I hadn't given it much effort.

So, I tried again the next year with a story called "The Lost Puppy." That story was about—wait for it—a *puppy* that gets lost in the forest. I know! This stuff writes itself! I drew pictures for that, too. And though this third-grade effort offered better description and a more heightened sense of tension, it didn't win either.

But I would not be deterred.

The *next* year, I challenged myself in a different genre altogether and decided to write poetry. And I illustrated that as well. Because, apparently, that was my thing. And that year, I made it as a runner-up.

So, my morale was back. Yet I sat out the contest in fifth grade—regrouped, I guess…waited for inspiration. I'm not sure. All I remember is that the following year I wrote "The Kid Next Door" and tasted greatness.

Okay, so, in retrospect, *that* story was pretty terrible, too. But that's not the point. When I wrote "The Panda's Lost Mother," I was a seven-year-old hack. I didn't want to write that story; I wanted to win the contest. It's like when I tried out for badminton freshman year at Elgin because I wanted the satin team jacket. And I got rejected for that, too!

But by the time I wrote poetry in fourth grade, I *wanted* to. I found actual joy in it. And then I *didn't* force myself to enter something the next year. I didn't write another story until one came to me that I actually wanted to write. And I think that's why, ultimately, the third and fourth times were the charm.

At the time, of course, I was just having fun. I wouldn't know what an important lesson I had learned until twenty years later when I began writing in earnest. But looking back on it now, I appreciate how every time I wrote and submitted a story to that contest, I made progress. I also failed, but then I tried again and got better.

I'm no stranger to rejection in my adult life either, but the more I've written and submitted my stories, the more rejections have turned into acceptances. It's a bit of a numbers game, but also a matter of growing in the craft. The greatest acceptance we could ever experience, though, is our *own* acceptance of our work. *We*, first and foremost, need to love it and feel proud of it. And if others don't love it, well then, we have to accept that, too.

I think it took me a while to learn that. As I outgrew my childhood moxie, I became more self-conscious as a writer. As of middle school and high school, I'd stopped entering writing contests, though I'm not sure if it was mostly lack of confidence or motivation. Probably a combination of both. I wasn't proactive like all of you seated here, contributing your lovely literary work to this festival, which is *so admirable*. I'm so proud and inspired by what you're accomplishing today.

What I can at least say for myself at your age is that, insecure as I was, I never stopped loving to write. I mean, yeah, I usually moaned over English assignments like everyone else, but whether it was a poem, short story, or essay, I truly did enjoy the challenge of crafting sentences in a way that would clearly and effectively communicate my message. I enjoyed figuring out what my message was in the first place. And I enjoyed playing with language, experimenting with turns of phrase. English is such a word-rich playground for that.

Which is why I loved, *loved* when my teachers would assign creative writing. My favorite task was when my sophomore English teacher gave us time in class to conduct freewritings. We had to keep a notebook solely for that, and she would give us something like five minutes to just write without stopping. Without caring about grammar or spelling or how weird our train of thought was getting. We just had to run with it, and it was the most liberating sensation, unlocking parts of my brain I didn't realize I had.

Twenty-five years later, I still distinctly remember Mrs. Morrison commenting in my notebook, "You have a poet's instinct for imagery." That's stuck with me. As does a professor's comment on one of my graduate-school essays. He'd said my writing was good, but it could be *great* if I just relaxed it a little.

And it did need relaxing. I always tried too hard, speaking more from my head than my heart, trying to sound intellectual, and saying in two words what I could've said in one. I hope you take *your* teachers' feedback to heart like I did, be it their compliments or criticism. Both are invaluable and neither should encourage you to either rest on your laurels or give up. Keep. Writing.

I wish *I* had kept writing creatively, but I'd let it lapse awhile during and after college, when I studied finance and became a consultant. In the years to follow, I wrote mainly emails and financial analysis. As all the while, my mother lamented, "Where are my writers? Where is my poet?" since all four of us kids had gone into either accounting or finance.

My brothers are still CPAs, but both my sister and I are now authors—so, Mom? *You're welcome.* My sister and I both started out in finance, too, and maybe we weren't *writing* fiction then, but we continued to *read* it as our escape from an everyday existence that paid the bills but didn't quite make us tick. I don't regret pursuing a business career—it's challenging and rewarding in its own way—but during those daily commutes to downtown Chicago, when I was reading a novel when I probably should've been keeping up to date with the *Wall Street Journal* or something, I just knew. I *knew* I wasn't long for the business world.

One day, I left the office to visit a bookshop. I was picking out a gift for a niece or nephew, looking through the children's section when I came across my all-time favorite picture book as a kid: *The Story of Ferdinand,* by Munro Leaf. I don't know if you've read it, but it's basically about a peaceful bull who loves smelling flowers more than anything. He chooses not to romp around with the other young bulls and won't fight inside the bullring in Madrid. He simply wants to sit under his favorite cork tree and smell the flowers.

Believe it or not, finding this book in that bookstore on that day was an epiphany for me. Standing between the shelves, flipping through this story that I hadn't read since childhood, I realized that I didn't want to fight the corporate bullfight anymore either. It went against my grain, and all I wanted was to find my way of smelling the flowers, too.

Which is when I realized: books. Books are my flowers. They always have been. Reading them, teaching them, now writing and editing them. My life's been a virtual greenhouse ever since I decided to pull a 180 and leave consulting to study English language and literature instead. I earned my master's in education and became an English teacher, first as a student teacher and long-term substitute at Geneva High School (go, Vikings!) and then as a full-time teacher here at St. Charles North (go, North Stars!). Teaching was by far the toughest job I've ever had, but I *loved* my work here. I loved my students and colleagues and the communities of the Upstate Eight. In my heart, this area will always be my home.

But life does happen. Nearly ten years ago, I got married and moved to London for my husband's career. I won't pretend the transition wasn't difficult, but now I'm a dual American and British citizen, and the UK has become another home, and another inspiration for writing.

And I'm talking *crazy* inspirational—I can't walk a block without stumbling on something of historical or literary significance. I live right down the street from where Beatrix Potter wrote her *Peter Rabbit* tales. I often stroll through Kensington Gardens, where *Peter Pan* was inspired, and I've explored Shakespeare's hometown. I've seen Charlotte Brontë's original manuscript for *Jane Eyre* and stood in Jane Austen's house. I've hung out at Charles Dickens' old haunts and met his great-great-*great*-granddaughter Lucinda Hawksley. I've even had one of my manuscript chapters critiqued in person by a descendant of Charles Darwin, the author Emma Darwin.

So, for close to a decade, I've been OMG-ing my fool head off over walking in the footsteps of my literary heroes, feeling ever humbled by their talent but ever aspiring to it.

Yet the fact of the matter is, moving to London did take me away from family, friends, and my teaching career here. That was heartbreaking. And though I started out teaching across the pond as a substitute, until I could find satisfactory full-time work, I blogged for a London relocation agency, writing about life in the UK from my expat perspective. Professional blogging was my first foray into writing at length every day, and I found the process of sharing my written experience very therapeutic. And since I only worked part-time, I finally had the opportunity to try what I'd always wanted to do: *write a novel*.

Oh, yeah, *suuure*. Write a novel. Simple.

Right. I had no clue how to come up with an idea that I could run with for the entire length of a book! But what I always consider first as a writer is: *What do I enjoy as a* reader? Probably the best advice I've ever received and could impart to you today is this: *Write what you want to read.*

Write what you want to read.

For me, that's fiction with elements of mystery, history, and a touch of the supernatural. Something modern but with a Gothic edge. Having lived in historic buildings in both Chicago and London, I can't help but think of all the lives that occupy the same spaces over the decades if not centuries. Living and dying there. I look around and imagine what might've happened in the rooms where I stand, where I sleep. So, the nature of time and the soul just fascinates me and can be explored through so many dimensions; I don't think I could ever exhaust all the ways to approach it.

But sometimes even all that possibility is overwhelming—almost scarier than having no clue what to write about. I might feel like my ambition exceeds my talent, and I psyche myself out. Which blocks me from writing.

To overcome a really bad bout of writer's block that I had on my first book, I turned to short fiction. I cracked open a journal and did freewriting like I used to in high school. I started a personal blog and posted my responses to writing prompts. I also took some of these entries and revised them to submit to flash-fiction sites and short-story contests. And I simultaneously began editing for a small publishing company, which helped me hone my craft by helping others.

And within a few years of trying, really *trying* to make space for writing in my life, I got two short stories and two novels published, mostly under the pen name Rumer Haven. Both novels are ghost stories of sorts that switch between past and present, and I'm currently wrapping up a 1920s murder mystery. After that, I'm tackling a paranormal book series, if all goes to plan, along with an anthology of supernatural stories. So, for as much as I've done, I've still got my work cut out for me.

Because let's not kid ourselves: Writing is a joy, but writing is also *a lot of work*.

Films would have people believe that we writers are reclusive, brooding creatures, feverishly scribbling with ink-stained fingers by candlelight, dashing off masterpieces in a burst of inspiration as our Muse sings softly in one ear and her sister strokes a harp in the other.

I know friends have found *my* life very Hemingway and romantic, the expat writer crafting stories in foreign cafés when I'm not at my typewriter up in a garret or a turret or something — when, in reality, I'm most often in my flat at the computer, wearing yoga pants — maybe a sock-monkey hat — squished into the tiny second bedroom that also triples as my office and my husband's closet. Writing is my work, so sometimes I just have to do what it takes to git 'er done. No frills.

Never mind getting published and marketing books after the fact — the writing and revising alone is work. All of it.

And that does psyche a lot of people out. Understandably so! What's more intimidating than staring down a blank computer screen or sheet of paper?

But whenever I'm asked for advice on how to start writing, my response is pretty basic: "Start writing." The only way to do it is to, you know, *actually do it*. You can't sculpt anything without the clay. There's nothing to polish and perfect without a first draft. A really rough, rambling, rookie first draft. That's what you cut your teeth on.

So, just write. Write about everything; write about nothing. Watch people and things; observe behavior and sensory detail. And when you first write something down about it, don't put the pressure on yourself to make it perfect. That all comes in due time. For now, just let go.

Getting in the habit of writing a little something every day warms you up and gets you into a groove. Stretching and flexing your creative muscles is just like exercising — the more you do it, the more energized you feel and the more you *want* to do it and inhibitions drop away.

I'll admit it: my own process isn't pretty. (Definitely not any prettier than me in a sock-monkey hat.) My creative process is messy and mental and just plain mean to me sometimes. Because all of my stories originate from a very scattered place: my brain. And the only way to get them out of my head is to kick up a windstorm in there and blow the ideas out onto paper.

And I do mean *paper*. I write my manuscripts on the computer, I do, but they always start as pen-to-paper. I don't know why, but something about the physical act of handwriting dislodges ideas in a way that typing at the computer does not. And, honestly, I don't even try to be organized about it — as soon as I have the bud of an idea, I go all-out brainstorming — writing any and all thoughts that come to mind onto any and all scraps of paper I can find — so then I can eventually look back at them from a bird's-eye view and begin connecting the dots.

From there, I tidy it all into an outline. Granted, nothing neatly divided into tiers of *A, B, C, 1, 2, 3* like I used to teach my students for five-paragraph essays. They're more like back-of-the-envelope bullet points, but guidance nonetheless. Just enough to give me a sense of the story's shape and direction without confining my creativity.

It's definitely different for everyone, but I personally need to allow for some organic flow, balancing structure with spontaneity. I wouldn't enjoy the writing process nearly as much if I plotted everything meticulously in advance. That gives me the breathing room I need to change my mind if I end up wanting to head somewhere else.

It also allows for those odd and wonderful moments of pure writing *magic*, when it's almost like the characters are whispering the next scenes in your ear. As if the story already exists on some level, independent of you, but *you've* been chosen to tell it. When this happens, it's a little haunting but so amazing. When, truly and almost inexplicably inspired, you just write without knowing where it's going and end up creating something better than it ever would've been if you'd thought about it too hard.

Those are the moments when writing feels easy. But since you can't force the magic, you need to *en*force the method.

Ultimately, you need to find the method that works best for *you*, and surely your process will evolve with experience, just as mine continues to. But even setting our own expectations requires *discipline* as we make time for our writing and revise it until it becomes the best version of itself.

I wish I could say that I write every day, but I don't. At least not creatively. Otherwise, sure, I'm writing. I write emails or text messages or social media posts (or keynote speeches). But creatively, some days I just don't feel it. The story goes quiet, and the characters don't speak to me.

Those are discouraging times, and I always feel guilty. Because we can't just sit around and wait for inspiration. We need to try to show up on the page in some way.

Sometimes I do so by revising what I've already written. Or, I take to pen and paper again to brainstorm. *Or*, I don't write anything at all but still think through my plots and characters away from the computer. I've had some great revelations hit me while I'm shampooing my hair in the morning or falling asleep at night. I've even gotten pages of material just from walking through the old Victorian cemetery near my flat and reading the gravestones.

So, whatever works. Go for a walk. Ride your bike. Sketch or color some pictures. Just because you're not literally writing doesn't mean you aren't still "writing" in your mind — just as long as you do at some point jot down your thoughts before you forget them. Even writing just five minutes a day is better than none. You wouldn't train for a marathon by running twenty miles your first day. You start small and do what you can to show up on the page.

Still, at those honest-to-goodness times when I feel too tapped out to create anything — well, then I show up on someone *else's* page.

I *read*.

I sincerely believe we cannot be good writers unless we're good readers. Every time we read, it's an investment in our writing. On one level, we can observe how other writers structure and develop their work and craft their language. On another level, we can simply lose ourselves in the *experience* of someone else's written world, rediscover the *joy* to be found in words and imagination to remind us why we're writing our own pieces and recharge us for when we're ready to return to them.

Because, why *do* we write? Why *should* we?

Anaïs Nin once said, "We write to taste life twice, in the moment and in retrospect."

That's a lovely sentiment, isn't it? *Tasting life twice*...what a sweet gift that writers get to enjoy.

Whether we're writing fiction or nonfiction, we draw from life experience in *some* way to fuel our work with authenticity and heart. Who we are impacts what we write as well as how we write it. You and five of your friends could look at the same tree and each describe it differently.

It's meaningful, not egotistical, to consider how your sense of self informs your writing. And it's when you stop being yourself in your writing that it can start sounding inauthentic and cliché.

Because, they always say, "Write what you know." And I agree with that, even though we have to write what we *don't* know. I mean, I don't know about you, but I've never been suspected of murder or haunted by a ghost. I haven't lived in Victorian London or 1920s Chicago. I've never been a twenty-five-year-old man or an eighty-year-old woman. For that matter, I've never been a panda or puppy lost in the forest! But I've written characters who are, which means I rely on research, observation, and imagination as much as experience. I have to know what I *don't* know, and then make the effort to know more about it.

Writing what we know isn't about writing our autobiographies. We can draw from events in our lives, but what we *know* is more about what we *feel*, how life experience has shaped us *emotionally*. We can harness that emotion to help us empathize with experiences outside of ourselves, and we can express it in a way that helps others empathize with us, too. The best way to engage our readers is to make them want to take the journey with us, inserting themselves into the experience even if they've never lived through anything like it either.

So, in tasting life twice, why *not* spice it up with more flavor? Why *not* challenge yourself to know what you don't know and expand on experience? In many ways, my real life has offered the inspiration I've needed to get started, yet the story inevitably evolves from there, trekking into terrain unlike anything I've personally known. I simply fit true elements into fictional contexts to communicate something entirely new. It's like dismantling a clock and using its gears to build a time machine.

Ernest Hemingway similarly said, "From all things that you know and all those you cannot know, you make something through your invention that is not a representation but a whole new thing truer than anything true and alive."

We also infuse authenticity into our writing through our powers of observation. For most folks, the world becomes too familiar as we age, losing more and more of the wonder it once held for us as children. Back when we questioned *everything*, were so curious about *all of the things.*

Writers, though, are blessed with the ability to hold on to that wonder. We notice subtleties, noticing people and how they behave, wondering where they're going or coming from, how they got that scar above their eyebrow or why they're smiling to themselves when they think no one's looking. We might notice a tree and think it looks kinda sad and lonely, or maybe something about it seems hopeful and safe. We notice with a painter's eye that clouds aren't just white or grey, or how the mood of a room shifts as the sun rises and sets. We notice what a gust of air feels like in our lungs, through our hair, and what it smells like, and what memories those scents can conjure. How the rustling leaves sound like a waterfall.

We behold the world with wonder, and not only are we richer for it, but we've been called to *write it down* so that others can see the world through our eyes and maybe notice it as if for the first time.

There's not always beauty in this awareness. We might instead reveal the darker side of humanity through gritty poems or prose. There might not be a happy ending. But there *will* always be Truth, so long as we write what we wonder at, and do so through our genuine voices and ability to empathize with what others might have to say, too. *That* is what makes our writing authentic and universal.

Unlike the negligent Dr. Frankenstein, however, we do need to be mindful of what we bring into being. Our writing inspires us, speaks to us, surprises us, yes, but it also relies on us to nurture and shape it, to find a suitable place in the world for it.

So, when you finish drafting your work, you're really *only just beginning*. Sorry to break it to ya. But luckily, editing is a creative process, too.

As your own editor, you need to be a "self-conscious" one. I don't mean self-conscious as in insecurity-ridden — I think we've all probably mastered that one just fine. What I mean is to *be conscious of the kind of writer you are and the audience you're writing for.*

Step back from your draft and look at it as a whole. Does it achieve what you want it to? Is this what you wanted to write? Also, is this what your readers will want to read? How will *they* experience it?

Because, we can't forget about the reader if we eventually want to share our work. Arguably eighty percent of its meaning will come from the reader, not us.

No matter how much they might lose themselves in our writing, readers still form their own interpretations based on *their* personal experiences and attitudes. So, we want to strike a chord with them through our work so they can make their own meaning from it.

In many ways, our writing is self-examination. We see ourselves in our words every step of the way. But consider, too, how our writing can hold a mirror up to our readers, confirming or challenging their perspectives and possibly showing them another way of living and thinking. As much as your writing might be for yourself, it could also help your readers make sense of themselves, others, and the greater world around us.

And while I'm on the topic of others reading our work, allow me to drill this into your heads:

Everyone needs an editor.

Everyone needs an editor.

Everyone needs an editor.

I stress this not only as a writer whose manuscripts desperately need editing, but as an *editor* who's prepared dozens of manuscripts for publication. Even the strongest stories with the strongest grammar need more work than you'd realize. Whether it's idea development, pacing, style, or the nitty-gritty of sentence construction and continuity, everything you write needs another set of eyes. For as solitary as the act of writing is, we can't do it alone.

Everything we write becomes our dear, sweet baby, and we can be ever so proud of it—and of ourselves—but it's downright diva to think we're above having our work critiqued. I know it's scary, though. Writing is such a personal passion. Such a vulnerable one. What we write is who we are, and who likes hearing they're anything less than perfect? So, frankly, every time we hand our work over to others, we're giving them the power to upset us.

It's hard to control how other people will respond to our writing, but we can control how graciously we respond to their feedback. It's okay to admit we're not perfect, and we'll never improve unless we accept our limitations by accepting help from others. I actually feel more confident knowing that. Because I know I'm not alone, and once I can own my weaknesses, I can work to strengthen them.

As an editor, it never ceases to amaze me how much easier it is to identify issues in someone else's manuscript than my own. As a writer, I'm simply too close to my story to see what others can. So, I welcome having my work edited. And I welcome editing others' work, even if it takes me away from my writing—because it's a thrill to help someone else share their story with the world, and I in turn learn so much from their talent and creativity.

Also, editing's not just fixing what we're doing *wrong* but learning what we're doing *right*. As a teacher and an editor, I have always balanced my criticism with positive feedback so that my students and authors feel good about their work and remain confident in their voices and what they have to say. That's why I end every editorial letter with this:

It's an act of great trust when a writer shares his or her work with someone else and opens it to commentary. I thank you for this trust and hope my feedback demonstrates an understanding of your work, your style, and what you're seeking to achieve.

Because here's the thing: no matter what, your writing *is* for yourself. Even when you're sharing it with the world. Keeping an audience in mind doesn't mean forgetting who you are at heart.

There's endless advice out there for what we writers should and shouldn't do. But, ultimately, there's no one-size-fits-all formula to writing a good story, sketch, narrative, essay, poem, or play. We each bring something unique to the craft, and that's something we should celebrate in our writing as well.

You can only be the writer you are. So, listen to your voice, and find *your* way of smelling the flowers.

Acknowledgments

I only have others to thank for the stories appearing in this collection. Without those outside nudges, almost of none of these tales would have existed—which perhaps would've been your preference, dear reader, but as for me, I'm very grateful to the following:

Bonni Goldberg and her *Room to Write* book of writing prompts, which saw me through writer's block and inspired me to start a creative writing blog, giving me some semblance of discipline on my initial path to publication. Ashley Horn of Bibliotheca Alexandrina, for accepting my very first story to ever be published. The online magazine that put the call out for urban-legend retellings; I cannot for the life of me remember your name, but you didn't accept my story anyway, so #sorrynotsorry. Michelle Devon of Twin Trinity Media, for awarding my contest submission with First Place, and Fawn Neun of Vagabondage Press, for later publishing it. Casey Wolfe and Jason T. Reed of Brick Moon Fiction, for their themed call for submission and generous permission to print "The Glass Floor" in this collection. Milton Liu, fellow writer and friend, for connecting me with Brick Moon and being an early encourager of my writing (yeah, you). Morgan and Jennifer Locklear of Locklear Books, for inviting me to contribute to their anthologies. And Shannon

Von Essen and Sue Schiller of St. Charles North High School, for approaching me to take part in their regional literary festival.

My sincerest gratitude also goes to my trusted beta readers and editors, including fellow authors Nicki Elson, Sarah Allan, and Shani Struthers. And many thanks again to Coreen Montagna (interior design) and Gina Dickerson (cover design) for making my books such beauties, inside and out!

As always, I owe everything that is good and great in my life to my family. In the first edition of this collection, compiled in the summer of 2020, I lamented how I wasn't able to see anyone in the States, grounded in the UK by a pandemic. As I wrote then, "I'd have loved to have worked on my edits at your dining room table, Mom and Dad, rather than my kooky quarantine setup here—but I'm grateful, at least, for all the long-distance chats I've gotten to have with you, my siblings, nieces, nephews, and in-laws." The gift of time is that this second edition does find me at my parents' dining room table, working on edits.

The tricky thing with time, though, is now my dad's the one who isn't here. Sitting at this table, hunched over my laptop, I can still hear the clip-clop of his slippers as he'd shuffle in from the kitchen to top up my coffee—to which I'd say, "Thanks, Flo," and promise him a good tip. He's still here in spirit, I know, topping up my heart with the love that never dies.

Thanks, Flo.

Much love and gratitude to my husband Ryan, too, for being the sole family I have overseas, having to see me through everything in everyone else's place. You have a big place of your own in my heart, of course, that has only grown bigger through this expat experience together.

I must also give thanks and affection to Flat 4 in Redcliffe Square, where my writing journey began and all these stories were written. For twelve years, you let my weird ideas bounce off your walls, and I continue to haunt you in spirit.

And to you, the lovely person who has taken a chance on me by reading this book. Extra points for sticking it out long enough to read the boring acknowledgments. I never know if my stuff is all that it's cracked up to be (I'm not even really sure who, if anyone, is cracking it up in the first place), but I do what I can, and you sure are something else for giving it a go. For that, I cannot thank you enough.

To everyone, I send my love and blessings. I said it in 2020, and I'll say it again in 2025: Cheers to your health, safety, and whatever gives you a sense of peace. Let's all be good to each other.

About the Author

Rumer Haven is probably the most social recluse you could ever meet. When she's not babbling her fool head off among friends and family, she's pacified with a good story that she's reading, writing, or revising — or binge-watching *Buffy*. A writer/editor hailing from Chicago, she presently lives in London with her husband and probably a ghost or two. Rumer has always had a penchant for the past and paranormal, which inspires her writing to explore dimensions of time, love, and the soul. Her award-winning work includes *Coattails and Cocktails* (First Prize Winner, 2018 *Red City Review* Book Awards) and *What the Clocks Know* (First Place Winner in General Fiction, 2017 *Red City Review* Book Awards).

Visit Rumer at:
www.rumerhaven.com
@RumerHaven

Novels by Rumer Haven

Coattails and Cocktails

A body clearly shaken, but not stirring...

Summer, 1929. Murder isn't on the menu when Chicago tycoon Ransom Warne hosts a dinner party at his country estate. But someone's a victim — and everyone's a suspect — when drinks and desires lead to disaster.

Hollywood starlet Lottie Landry has returned home to celebrate her engagement. She's famous for her on- and off-screen romance with co-star Noble, but, privately, she's having second thoughts. As her former guardian, Ransom doesn't approve of the match. Yet his own affections raise questions when his wife, Edith, suspects him of having an affair — just as Noble suspects Lottie. Stirred into the mix are Lottie's friends Helen and Rex, a young journalist and football hero who can feel tension building in the Warne mansion like a shaken champagne bottle.

And once the cork pops, a body drops.

Coattails and Cocktails is where Agatha Christie meets *The Great Gatsby*, a whodunit spiked with new love and old baggage, public faces and private vices. Filled to the brim with romance and mystery, it's sure to intoxicate.

Seven for a Secret

It's the year 2000, and twenty-four-year-old Kate moves into a new apartment to find a new state of independence in a new millennium. Almost immediately, she starts crushing on a hot guy who lives in her building. Deciding to take a break from her boyfriend Dexter, Kate believes the only thing now separating her from the fresh object of her sexual fantasies is the thin wall between their neighboring apartments.

A former 1920s hotel, Camden Court has housed many lonely lives over the decades — and is where a number of them have come to die. They're not all resting in peace, however, including ninety-year-old Olive, who dropped dead in Kate's apartment and continues to make her presence known.

For Olive has a secret she's *dying* to tell. One linking her to the sex, scandal, and sacrifice of a young dreamer named Lon. As the past haunts the present, Kate's romantic notion that the thrill-of-the-chase beats the reality-after-the-catch unexpectedly entwines her modern-day love life with Lon's Jazz Age tragedy.

With a little supernatural and a lotta' razzle-dazzle, *Seven for a Secret* is where historical fiction meets contemporary rom-com — from the Roaring Twenties when the "New Woman" was born, to the modern Noughties when she really came of age.

What the Clocks Know

Suffering a quarter-life crisis, twenty-six-year-old Margot sets out on a journey of self-discovery—she dumps her Boston boyfriend, quits her Chicago job, and crosses the ocean to crash at her friend's London flat.

Rather than find herself, though, she only feels more lost. An unsettling energy affects her from the moment she enters the old Victorian residence, and she spirals into depression. Frightened and questioning her perceptions, she gradually suspects her dark emotions belong to Charlotte instead.

Who is Charlotte? The name on a local gravestone could relate to Margot's dreams and the gray woman weeping at the window.

Finding a ghost isn't what she had in mind when she went "soul searching," but somehow Margot's future may depend on Charlotte's past.

Woven between the nineteenth and twenty-first centuries, *What the Clocks Know* is a haunting story of love and identity that won First Place in General Fiction in the 2017 *Red City Review* Book Awards.